To my husband, Raffaele - who has always done his best to appreciate the music of my life - and to my children: Ken, Katie and Scott - who have always been eager to share their music with us at a reasonable volume;

to all of my friends for indulging me in my enthusiasm for new projects and ideas, with particular thanks to Suzanne for her encouragement to follow my dreams;

to my brother Marc whose spontaneous offer to design the cover nearly moved me to tears;

to my mother for making me;

I humbly and warmheartedly dedicate this book.

I0542795

Table of Contents

An introduction by the author

Autumn Sonata

A story in four movements:

An introduction by the author

Few novels require comment; this one does. I started this piece as an experiment, an exercise in style. As the story took shape, I knew it would be a good piece, one I would want to share with others. This short novel was conceived as a sonata for two instruments—clarinet and pianoforte.

The story is told in four movements:

I. Allegro appassionato

II. Andante un poco adagio

III. Allegretto grazioso

IV. Vivace

The chapters within each section represent changes in the music and therefore do not follow traditional rules of thumb for breaks in the story. The main characters are the musical instruments. Emily is the clarinet. Simon is the pianoforte. The events, dialogues, and interactions with other characters are the musical notes, all of which blend to achieve my indications for the tempo of the movement.

A sonata is a musical composition divided into three or four related but contrasting movements for one or two instruments. Generally speaking, the principal theme is introduced in the first movement. The remaining movements may contain hints of the theme, but it is usually not repeated again until the final movement, when it is presented to the audience in its final variation. In the case of this novel, the intense physical relationship between Emily and Simon represents the main theme.

The reader should try to imagine the scenes in which the main characters are not together as solo pieces, both instruments playing together only in those scenes in which Emily and Simon are together. The first movement, *Allegro appassionato* (translation: *lively with passion*), starts out lightly, alternating between clarinet and piano, which then blend to form the melody building in crescendo, represented by the couple's lovemaking. The movement ends with a brief clarinet solo as Emily returns home.

The second movement, *Andante un poco adagio* (translation: *moderately slow to slow and graceful*), is, as the tempo implies, soft and slow, taking its time to reach a climax. The melancholy solo of the clarinet is repeated by the development of the piano followed by an ensemble piece that recalls the first theme followed by a short virtuosic solo in clarinet that ends on a solitary discordant note. The story takes the reader back in time and traces the paths that brought Emily and Simon together.

In contrast to the second movement, in the third movement, *Allegretto grazioso* (translation: *somewhat lively, graceful*), the piano states and carries the main theme. The third movement starts out with a brief intense clarinet solo that picks up on the last note of the second movement, gradually becoming light and airy with the introduction of the piano. The almost playful melody played by the two instruments graciously accompanies the reader to the end of the movement.

The final movement is *Vivace* (translation: *very lively, quick*). As the tempo indication suggests, the final section of the book is an intense mixture of emotions and events.

The idea of transposing a musical structure to a work of literature is not new. Irene Nemirovsky used the same technique when writing her *Suite Française*. This was one of the main inspirations for my work. I was captivated by her endeavor. Her storyline certainly contributed to the success of the novel. A suite is an ensemble of musical pieces for dance. The fact that her characters were all in movement made it easier for her to transpose the musical structure onto the written page.

Music, when it isn't about physical movement like dance, is about expressing emotions. I knew, when I sat down to this exercise, that I needed a strong human emotion to help carry the musical theme. That is why I chose a love story. The intense physical relationship between the two protagonists was fundamental to the development of the sonata concept. If you listen to a sonata, the main theme is generally introduced in the first movement. It is richly embellished and played at some length so that the listener recognizes the bits and pieces of it that are reintroduced in other sections under different forms. The reader will note that I never go into that amount of detail again until the final movement and even then it is a much different description.

Although the structure of the novel was inspired by the structure of an existing sonata, Brahms' *Sonata for Clarinet and Piano Op. 120, No. 1*, the music itself did not inspire me. The Autumn Sonata does not really exist and, to the best of my knowledge, has not been written yet.

Allegro appassionato

Emily tried to focus on the speaker's voice, but she could feel a rising sense of tension in the pit of her stomach. For the past hour she had listened to the group of men seated at the long table at the front of the room as they espoused their ideas on policies and programs to promote women's role in economic development, and she had stomached just about all that she could hear on the subject.

She had been reluctant to attend this particular session at the World Economic Development Summit, but the other roundtable discussions being addressed that day interested her even less. She was there for the session on sustainability, but that topic wasn't on the agenda until tomorrow.

Emily sighed. This was her first time at the summit. There was no doubt that it was an important networking event and she had already had occasion to exchange business cards with several key decision makers including the vice president of Project Development for the World Development Bank. That was the main reason she had agreed to attend the summit. The company needed to start opening doors in the international financing world. Given the global economic crisis, it was imperative to tap into international development financing in order to guarantee that her company had a fighting chance of survival in the current market.

Granted, it wasn't an easy task. The company wasn't as big as most of its competitors and didn't really have the manpower to do the necessary lobbying to be considered as a technical consultant to help draft project specifications. As a result, the projects were almost always written around one of the company's competitors' products. It was frustrating, but that was business.

Emily tried to focus back on the speaker. The roundtable discussion was coming to an end and the moderator was about to open the session for questions and comments from the floor. Emily let her eyes skim the room briefly. She wasn't really aware that she was counting the women in the room until she realized with a start that there were only six, seven including herself. A wave of irritation drove the tension that had been lining the pit of her stomach to the tips of her fingers. She almost curled her hands into fists. She took a deep breath to release the tension. She wasn't angry. Emily rarely got angry. It was one of her better qualities.

Impulsively, she raised her hand to take the floor. The moderator saw her hand go up and smiled in acknowledgment, but another hand had gone up before hers, a young man, probably a college student, and the young woman handling the microphone had passed the mike over to him before the moderator could speak.

The young man didn't have a question, and it wasn't really clear what his point was. He obviously liked the sound of his own voice. The moderator let him speak for a few minutes. When it became blatantly obvious that he wasn't going to get to the point, the moderator interrupted the young man's flow of words and tried his best to summarize what he thought the young man had been trying to say, formulating a question for one of the panelists.

The question was an interesting one, although after an hour of discussion, one would have thought that the answer had already been given: "Why was empowering women so important to economic development?"

The five men at the table politely began inviting each other to answer the question. Finally, one of the men—Emily read his name, Simon Russell—cleared his throat and began to speak, "The answer to that question is really quite simple." His tone was slightly condescending, and his response was almost college textbook. "With very few exceptions, women represent the majority of the population in many developing countries. China, for example, is an exception, but in several African nations women account for nearly sixty percent of the overall population. That is an enormous wealth of potential to tap into and, of course, if you don't tap into that, the downside would be that you would have to provide for their wellbeing through social services, placing significant economic burden on government budgets in countries that don't really have much of a budget to begin with."

The moderator smiled at Emily, "There was a question at the back of the room." He indicated Emily and suddenly the microphone was in Emily's hand. As she took it, she realized that her hands were shaking slightly. For a VP in Corporate Marketing, she was incredibly shy and she still wasn't really sure what she was going to say as she stood up. She looked at the men seated at the front of the room.

There was something about the polite, politically correct smiles painted on their faces that gave her the impetus to speak. "Actually, I don't really have a question, but I would like to comment on," she paused, "today's discussion. Many of the programs and policies that have been expressed here today are interesting, but I was surprised to note that none of them addressed the fundamental issue facing women today: their safety. It's an issue that we still seem to have difficulty addressing in the western hemisphere, and I know that because I was raped when I was six years old."

Emily really hadn't been planning on stunning the crowd, but the silence that met her comment was total. Suddenly, the men on the podium weren't smiling. Several of them looked extremely uncomfortable. Emily noted that one of the speakers rolled his eyes and she could almost read his thoughts. She thought, "He thinks I'm going to go into a tirade."

Emily continued, "I realize that's a very uncomfortable thought, but I actually consider myself lucky because I grew up in a society that was able to help me grow out of the trauma." Emily drew a deep breath. "I think most of us know what the social conditions for women are in other countries. We've heard enough about them in the discussions today to form a clear picture, but I would like the decision makers in this room to reflect on the following. Creating a safe environment for women is no different than ensuring access to the diversely disabled or guaranteeing equal rights. Economic programs alone are not going to solve the problem. If you provide interest-free loans to women to start a business where they can still be raped or maimed or sold like cattle…they will probably only learn that money can't buy them happiness. We shouldn't confuse economic development, or even policy, with empowerment. One only has to look around this room to understand the truth in that statement. There are approximately seven women in this room. I don't mean to be rude but, frankly speaking, most of what I have heard here today was patronizing and superficial."

At this point, Simon Russell interrupted, "I'm sorry you feel that way and I agree with you that economic solutions alone won't solve all the problems facing women today, but I'm afraid I'm going to have to throw the comment back at you. You haven't given us any concrete example of ways you think the policies could be improved. Most of us have been working on this issue for over fifteen years now, and I'm sure we'd be delighted to hear your answer to the problem if you would like to share it with us. At the moment, it just really sounds as though you have an issue with men, which is understandable, of course."

"Mr. Russell. Did it ever occur to you that many of the women you are trying to help may have an issue with men?"

"Your point being?"

"My point being that I don't know enough about the individual programs you've highlighted today to discuss any of them in detail, but I haven't heard anything here today that convinces me, despite your affirmation to the contrary, that you do either," Emily handed the microphone back to the attendant.

There was a very uncomfortable silence and then several hands in the audience went up at once. The moderator looked at his watch and decided it was probably better to end the session rather than open the floor to the debate he could see forming.

Emily barely made it to the end of the aisle where she had been sitting when she was accosted by a petulant elderly gentleman with white hair, double chin, and double-breasted jacket. Emily smiled politely as he waxed poetic about his commitment to women's economic development, expounding his years of work in Africa and his expertise. He was so verbose, Emily found herself struggling to pay attention. Somewhere at the back of her mind, she could hear her more cynical side wondering whether or not he had had air conditioning in his office in Nairobi.

Simon hadn't planned on giving the woman from his session a second thought. He was becoming a veteran on the speaker circuit. Knowledgeable, charismatic, and athletically built, he tended to dominate every conference he participated in. His easy confidence and calm ability to establish rapport with people across the globe had taken him far in his career and, at forty-five, he was a well-established policy advisor and consultant. He was currently working as chair for one of the United Nation's many subcommittees for economic development.

Simon had quickly classified the woman's observations as a mild case of sour grapes. He got that all the time in his field. He had focused briefly when she mentioned her childhood trauma but, since it seemed irrelevant, had quickly dismissed the fact and had only fleetingly registered that she was questioning his expertise because, behind the façade, Simon was already busy working on the report he had to submit to the steering committee the following week; Simon was slightly nonplussed to find himself standing next to her in line at the luncheon buffet. He had just decided that the best policy would be to ignore her when she spoke, "Excuse me. Mr. Russell?"

Simon sighed and turned to her with a polite expression.

Emily smiled as she read his face. "I should probably apologize. I'm not really good at extemporizing my thoughts. I think I've just actually been to too many conferences of this type. You get a bit tired of hearing the same thing over and over again. It makes you wonder whether or not the problems have been formulated correctly. I guess that's the point I wanted to get across. I found several of your comments very insightful, actually."

Simon really didn't know what to say, but Emily saved him the trouble by flashing him a kind smile and walking away. Simon couldn't help noticing that she had a very tight ass. Her legs weren't bad either and he liked the way she was dressed.

After lunch, Simon found himself sipping coffee in the lounge waiting for the afternoon sessions to begin when Emily walked into the lounge and up to the bar. Simon registered her arrival out of the corner of his eye. His mind was really on the papers in front of him but she caught his attention when he heard her speak in Italian to the waiter behind the bar. At least he thought it was Italian. The waiter's name was Antonio so it was a fairly good guess. It certainly wasn't Turkish. Simon watched as the waiter prepared an espresso. The two exchanged pleasantries and Simon found himself enjoying the scene. She had a very nice laugh. He wondered what they were talking about. Simon shook himself a bit. He didn't even know her name and he had work to do. He went back to his paperwork. When he looked up ten minutes later she was gone. Simon worked for another hour and then decided it was time to go to the session on creative financing. He had promised Susan he would sit in on the session.

Emily had spent the entire afternoon debating which sessions she would attend in the afternoon. The decision to attend the creative financing session had been spur of the moment. The room was already full. The only seats available were in the last row. Emily slid into the first seat available and settled down to listen to the debate. Simon arrived even later than Emily did and had to stand. Luckily, this was a short session. As Simon listened, he let his eyes roam the room. She was so close that he hadn't noticed her right away. Someone's cell phone rang, and Emily turned to see who it was. Her profile caught briefly in the light from the television camera that was panning the audience and Simon had to grudgingly admit that she had a pleasant face. He began to think about what she had said at lunchtime about hearing the same thing over and over again and whether or not the problem had been formulated properly. He was startled out of his thoughts by the sudden movement of everyone getting up to leave at the end of the session. He shook his head slightly and waded his way through the crowd to greet Susan. He could see her at the front of the room talking to one of the speakers.

Simon actually had a very high opinion of women. He had been married to one for fifteen years. Susan, his ex-wife, was still one of his best friends even though he didn't see her often. They had both gone their separate ways after the divorce. Both of them were working on the international circuit and their paths rarely crossed. That had been one of the main reasons they had gotten divorced. Simon had been devastated when Susan had asked for a divorce.

He had been comfortable with their relationship and had been brought up to believe that marriage was forever, but he had adjusted to being single again more quickly than he thought possible. He and Susan had spent so much time apart that, if he was honest with himself, he barely noticed the change.

Five years later neither one of them had remarried. Susan was living with her current boyfriend and, from the short conversation Simon had had with her, it seemed like the relationship was getting serious. Simon had dated a few women but still hadn't met anyone he wanted to get that emotionally involved with—not that he was ever in any one place long enough for that to happen. This past year and a half he had tried a few one-night stands on the conference circuit. Susan had chided him about that, but he had feigned indifference, saying it was only sex between two consenting adults in need. Susan had given him one of those penetrating looks that said, *I know you better than that*, but if she had had anything else to say on the subject she kept it to herself.

"Hey there. How's my favorite strawberry?" Simon hugged his ex-wife.

"Simon. In case you haven't noticed, I'm no longer strawberry blonde. I've gone amber."

Simon laughed. "You were never my favorite strawberry for the color of your hair. You smell like a strawberry and you squish like one, too."

"Thanks a lot. Are you implying that I'm fat?"

"Absolutely not. Just pleasantly plump."

"Humph. No wonder you haven't found anyone. Your charm is impossible. And I do mean impossible!"

Susan was laughing at him but Simon didn't mind. It was always the same with her. He liked the light banter. It was refreshing. "So how is Richard?"

"Very good. Actually, he'll be flying in tomorrow afternoon. We're going to stay on for the weekend and enjoy Istanbul."

"Tomorrow afternoon. Oh joy. Listen, don't be too offended, but Jeffrey has invited me to the embassy for dinner tomorrow night so if you were planning on a threesome for dinner or something like that, it's not going to happen."

"Richard feels the same way about you. I think that's why he's flying in so early."

"Jealous of the ex?"

"Probably."

"Well, it's not like I never gave it a thought, but after five years...I almost feel like we're brother and sister."

"Nice try."

"You're not buying?"

"When you present me with the future Mrs. Russell, maybe I'll believe you."

Simon grimaced. "Mind if we change the subject?"

"Sure. How did your roundtable go? Rob told me he had to cut the question-and-answer session short."

" Hmm. It was fairly routine."

"You had to think before you said that. What happened?"

"One of the, shall we say, seven women in the audience got up, and I think she very politely told us we were full of shit."

Susan laughed. She had a hearty laugh that reminded Simon briefly of the light laugh he had heard earlier that afternoon. "How does one politely say you're full of shit?"

"I'm not sure. I'm still thinking about it. I ran into her at the buffet afterwards and she apologized, but…"

"But?"

"But I don't think she really did. She said she thought she'd been to too many of these conferences and it's always the same thing over and over again."

"Ouch."

"Ouch is right. "

"Wound the ego a bit?"

"No! But something else she said has touched a nerve. She said it made her wonder whether or not the problem had been formulated correctly."

"And that touched a nerve because…?"

"Because when you reach forty-five years of age and you've been working on the same issue for the past fifteen years without much progress, you do begin to question whether or not you were right to begin with."

"Wow. You know, Simon, that's the first time in all the years that I've known you that something someone has said has actually gotten to you."

Simon was miffed. "I think it's more of a midlife crisis than anything else."

"Could be, but now I'm curious. You're going to have to point this woman out to me. I want to have a chat."

"Susan. I assure you, I'm not interested. She's definitely not my type."

"You never know."

Simon changed the subject. "So. What's on the menu for the gala dinner tonight?"

"The chef calls it Turkish fusion. A mixture of Mediterranean and traditional Turkish dishes, but wait until you see the restaurant. It's on the top floor and the patio has a bird's eye view of Istanbul that is absolutely breathtaking."

"Assigned seating?"

"Of course. You know, as one of the organizers, I could make some last minute changes if you wanted to sit by…"

"Put a lid on it Susan. Just promise me that Raj isn't at my table. You know he isn't one of my favorite persons."

"Already taken care of." At that point Susan's cell phone rang. It was Richard. Susan's whole face lit up. She smiled at Simon, cupped his chin briefly, and then walked away using her free hand to signal that she would see him later.

Simon watched her back as she walked away. It pained him that he really didn't remember her walk anymore. As her wriggling backside disappeared from view, Simon sighed. He wasn't in love with Susan anymore. He wasn't even slightly attracted by her, but every time he saw her he was reminded of the void she had left in his life. He didn't have anyone he could call on his cell phone for a bit of light banter or phone sex or even a fight. It was 5:20. Dinner was at 8:00. Simon decided he would check his emails, head to the gym for a workout, and then pick up where he had left off on his report. He turned and left the room. The lights on the podium went out behind him.

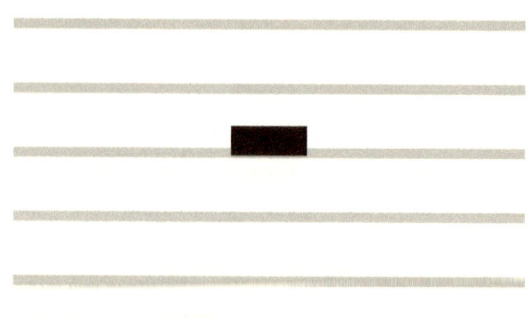

Emily laughed self-consciously as she crossed paths with Simon Russell at the gym door. She had already finished her workout and was embarrassed by her sweaty appearance. "It figures we'd be synchronized today. I just hope I don't become your worst nightmare."

Her eyes were dancing mischievously behind her glasses as she looked up at him, but she was gone before he could even formulate an answer.

He caught a brief glimpse of her leg as it disappeared through the door. Nice calf. He couldn't quite put an age to her. If he had to guess he would have said forty, but he never had been very good at guessing women's ages. He got on the treadmill, hit the automatic aerobic workout, checked that the settings were his usual workout settings, and started the machine.

Emily breathed a sigh of relief as she got off the elevator. How embarrassing to run into someone like that in the gym. That was why she usually did her workout in her room. Emily was an attractive middle-aged woman, forty-six to be exact. It was hard to believe that she was the mother of three. She had a tiny waist and small breasts, definitely not the matronly type. She had a fair amount of cellulite on the backs of her legs, but she usually wore knee-length skirts and shorts that hid that part of her body. She worked hard to keep herself in shape, but she was never satisfied with her body, or herself for that matter.

Life hadn't been kind to her. She had been raped at the age of six and, at home, she had had to put up with an extremely violent father and an alcoholic mother. She wasn't able to get out of that vicious cycle until she was eighteen. A college scholarship had been her ticket out of hell. She had studied hard to maintain her grade point average and had worked nights in a pizza parlor to pay her other expenses. After college, she had gone to Europe as an English language assistant. Twenty years later, she was married to an Italian and living in a small town in northern Italy.

It hadn't been something she had planned on, but that was the way that life had turned out. As a woman and a foreigner in Italy, she had had a very slow climb up the corporate ladder. That hadn't really posed a problem to her since it had given her a chance to have a family her way. Her children were her entire universe. Everything she did, she did thinking of them. Whenever she had to travel for work, she felt physically ill at the thought of leaving them behind, despite the fact that they were now old enough to understand and, as teenagers, were probably pretty happy not to have their mother hovering over them.

Emily took a long shower. When she got out of the shower, the phone was ringing.

"Hi, Mom."

"Benjamin! How's it going on the home front?" Benjamin was her eldest son. He was seventeen.

"Nothing special at this end. Erica had another fight with Dad yesterday because she wanted to go to town in her short shorts. Toby keeps sneaking onto the computer to watch his Star Wars movies."

"Sounds like everything is under control. What about dinner?"

"Erica made a spinach pie."

"Yum. We've got a gala dinner tonight. Hopefully the dress I brought with me will be adequate."

"Huh? Oh, Dad just came in. He wants to talk to you."

"Put him on."

"Hi. How's it going?"

"Wish I could see something of the city. It looks fascinating from the hotel window. Other than that, I've been busy at the conference. I did manage to find a nice outfit at the hotel boutique during the lunch break."

"I thought you said you weren't going to buy any more clothes for awhile."

"Wait until you see it."

"Is it a sexy pajama ensemble?"

Emily flinched. "No."

"Hmm. Then I'm not particularly interested."

"Was there something else you wanted to say?" Emily found her voice tensing despite herself.

"What's the weather like?"

"Nice. It was cloudy this morning but then the sun came out. The temperature is perfect. It's like an Indian summer."

"When are you coming home?"

"On Saturday morning. I'll take a taxi from the airport."

"Okay. I have to work anyway."

"Again? That's the third Saturday in a row. Does Toby want to talk to me?"

"I don't know. Toby! Your mother is on the phone. Pick up the phone."

"Hi, Mom."

"Hi, baby. How are you?"

Emily chatted with her youngest son, catching up on his day, and then asked if Erica wanted to speak with her. Erica, of course, was still angry over her fight with her dad and didn't want to speak with her mother. Emily sighed and wished everyone a good night.

It was 7:30. Time to get ready for dinner.

Emily was careful with her hair and makeup. She rarely wore makeup but on an occasion like this she felt it was necessary. For once, her hair was actually behaving itself, and she was satisfied with her appearance as she took a final look at herself in the mirror. She gathered her purse, checked that she still had the dinner invitation and the room key, and then left her room.

She rode up to the restaurant alone.

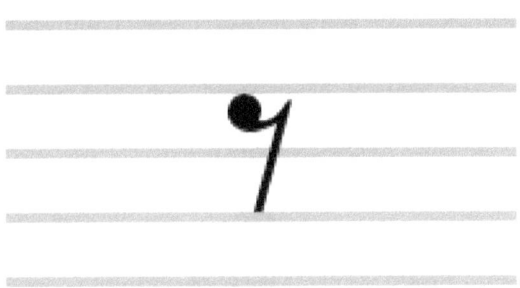

Simon was one of the last to arrive. The room was crowded with elegantly clad men and women chatting pleasantly and sipping on glasses of sparkling white wine. Susan caught sight of him almost the minute he stepped off the elevator. She had been waiting for him and was now making a direct beeline in his direction. Simon smiled and waited for her in the entry to the restaurant. He recognized the look on her face. She had something important she wanted to say; she wasn't exactly smiling. When she reached him, she said, "Emily White."

"Sorry?"

"Emily White. Your mystery lady. The woman from your afternoon session. Her name is Emily White."

"Susan. What on earth have you been up to? I told you to let it drop. I'm not interested."

"I don't care whether you are or not. I was curious, but that's not the point. Anyway, she's married and the mother of three, and she doesn't strike me as the type for a one-night stand. The point is that Emily White is head of corporate marketing at one of Italy's largest multinationals, and she's one of our special guests this year. We were hoping to convince her to sponsor next year's summit. I had made arrangements to seat her at our table, as a matter of fact. I thought between the two of us that we might be able to win her over. I just spent the last half hour rearranging the seating, and it hasn't been easy. You're lucky I didn't put Raj at your table. It would have served you right."

"Hey. Would you mind telling me how this is suddenly all my fault?"

Susan gave a slight exasperated sigh. "It's not your fault. It's just…if she thinks the summit is the same old, same old, I've got an uphill battle ahead of me to woo her over. And I was really counting on your help."

Simon looked down at Susan slightly amused. "If it's any help, she thought some of my comments were insightful."

"Now you tell me. Well, it's too late now. I've moved the two of us to table nine with Jason. You're at table ten."

"You're abandoning me?"

"Not abandoning you. I did that five years ago, anyway."

"Ouch."

"Simon. Behave yourself. You've got a great table, actually. I put most of my best conversationalists at table ten. This is business. I think it would be better to have some face-to-face time with Ms. White. Get to know her better. She mentioned she was interested in the session on sustainable development tomorrow, so I'm hoping Jason can draw her into a conversation about her expectations for the roundtable. He's going to be moderating tomorrow and he's good at piloting debates. He's also young and very cute."

"You know, you are really devious sometimes."

"Not devious. Just desperate. We need funding."

"Doesn't everyone these days."

"Anyway, if you lean back in your chair, you should be able to hear our conversation. We're only going to be about a foot and a half away. It was a tight squeeze to get everyone in tonight. We're at maximum capacity."

"Why on earth would I want to eavesdrop on your conversation?"

"Give me a break. She makes a passing comment that sends you into an existential crisis and your eyebrows practically met your hairline when I told you she was head of corporate marketing. You're curious."

Simon let out a short quick chuckle, pulling his ex-wife to his side and putting his arm around her in order to pilot her into the room and toward the bar. "Suz, you're impossible! And, you read too much into things. My eyebrows went up because she doesn't fit my stereotype of the corporate manager type. You know, power suite, short sassy haircut, platinum blonde hair. She's actually fairly average."

"Average?" Susan laughed and rolled her eyes theatrically. "Oh, a pox on all women. You obviously haven't taken a good look at her. Wait until you see her tonight. She's gorgeous. She's got really great taste in clothes—must be all those years of living in Italy. Jason's taken her out onto the patio to show her the view. But seriously, getting back to the subject, you are just as curious as I am to know what she's really thinking and how her brain works."

Simon barely heard the tail end of her conversation; he was already removing his arm from around her waist to greet the man coming towards them. "Enrique. Como estas?"

For the next fifteen minutes, Simon was caught up in his conversation with Enrique. Several other men joined in and since they all knew each other fairly well, the conversation flowed smoothly and freely from one topic to another. Simon didn't even notice Susan had left his side and was startled when the waiter appeared in her place, inviting the gentlemen to move from the bar into the dining area.

They arrived at their respective tables together. Jason Black was just pulling Emily's chair out for her to sit down but, as that would have blocked Simon's access to his place at the table, he pushed the chair back in to let Simon pass. Emily turned so that she was facing him and smiled as though she were enjoying some private joke. Simon slid by her. His eyes couldn't help following the curve of her neckline, which was just low enough and tight enough to evidence that there were small high breasts beneath the cloth. His nose picked up the scent of her perfume. It was so delicate he almost wasn't sure it was there. He certainly never would have noticed it if they hadn't been that close.

For a fraction of a second he was intoxicated and then it was gone. He was pulling his chair out and sitting down. He watched Emily do the same. The chairs had been staggered like the teeth on a gear, so Simon could see Emily's full profile as she sat down. Susan was right. If you ignored the glasses, Emily White was very attractive and very tastefully dressed. Instinctively, his eyes moved to Emily's left, where his ex-wife was taking her seat. She was looking straight at him with a look that said, *I told you so.*

Simon raised his eyes briefly to the ceiling, as if in surrender, then turned his entire attention to the people seated at his table, determined to enjoy the evening.

Emily White was not good at extemporizing her opinion; she was too introverted. Moreover, she was shy and reserved, but she was also an acute judge of character with a quick intelligent mind. It had taken her all of five seconds to recognize Susan's sales strategy, but that was probably because she had been expecting it ever since she had received their invitation to attend the summit.

Emily appreciated the subtlety. There was nothing pushy in Susan's approach. Emily was also highly amused by Jason Black's flattery. Emily guessed that Jason was in his mid- to late thirties. He still retained the enthusiasm of his youth. He was also very sure of himself, almost cocky. He had boyish good looks that reminded Emily of a puppy, and it was fairly evident that he thought he could rely on his charm in any situation.

He was totally out of his league with Emily the minute he started on the topic of sustainable development. Jason's knowledge was basically textbook, college level. Emily had years of experience on her side. Jason didn't give up his side of the argument despite several attempts on Susan's side to change the subject. On the pretext that she had to check on her guests, Susan got up from the table. She wormed her way around the back of the table to where Simon was sitting, deep in conversation. She leaned in over the table, placing her hand nonchalantly on his shoulder to ask everyone how they were doing. She stood there chatting pleasantly with everyone and then turned to go, squeezing Simon's shoulder slightly as she did so. That was her signal that she wanted to talk with him. He glanced over to where Jason was animatedly trying to drive home his argument. Simon didn't know what they were talking about. He had done a very good job of ignoring them. He thought he could detect a slight air of amusement on Emily's face but he wasn't sure.

Susan had made her way to the bar by this time. Simon sighed inwardly to himself and then excused himself from the table, worming his way around the back of the table rather than passing behind Emily's chair. The restrooms were situated in the hallway just to the right of the entrance to the restaurant as you went out. Susan bided her time at the table nearest the bar, timing it so that she arrived casually at the restaurant entrance at the same time as Simon.

"Phew. Jason is way out of his league. Actually, I don't think there's a man in this room who could keep up with her. No offense. She's sharp, and she's obviously very knowledgeable. I'm not getting anywhere."

"Is that what you dragged me over here to tell me?"

"I thought you might want to know that there is nothing casual about her comments. Whatever it was she said to you, she meant it. You should hear some of the things she's said to Jason this evening. It's almost painful to watch. She's so polite and soft-spoken that he's absolutely clueless, but she's pointed out the flaws in his logic so many times that I almost feel embarrassed for him. I'm half tempted to pull him off the session tomorrow as moderator."

Simon glanced to where Emily was sitting. "She doesn't look like she's not enjoying herself, Suz. Just write it off as experience and make the most out of the evening. You've outdone yourself this time. Could do with a little more water on the tables but the food is fantastic and so is the location. Everyone is having a good time. Go easy on yourself. You win some, you lose some."

Susan growled through her teeth. "That's easy for you to say. You've got a slew of organizers out there ready with big fat paychecks for your appearance at their events. I need new sponsors to help keep this event alive and pay for my *quality* speakers." She emphasized the word quality with a distinct tone of chagrin before turning back to her other guests.

Simon smiled at her back and then proceeded to the restroom because he suddenly realized that he really did need to go.

Simon took his time in the men's room. He was actually feeling very relaxed. It wasn't until the waiter had poured him his third glass of wine somewhere between the second and third courses that he realized he had already gone past his two-glass limit. Simon wasn't a drinker. He liked a good glass of wine every once in awhile, especially with a nice evening meal, but, as a rule, he never had more than two glasses. Simon had left the glass of wine where the waiter had poured it and had switched to water, but the room was warm and the food was spicy, so when the water ran out he had been forced to pick the wine back up. He knew he wasn't drunk but his guard was definitely down.

As he made his way back to his table, he noted that Susan was talking animatedly to Jason over an empty chair. Emily White had obviously left the room. Simon shrugged his shoulders and made his way back to his seat and sat down. His eyes lit up as he noticed the fresh bottle of water standing in front of his plate. Susan was very good at her job. The meal was coming to an end. The waiters were clearing off the last of the dinner dishes to make room for dessert. Several of the people from his table were now on their feet, speaking to other guests at tables around the room. Simon reached forward and took the dinner menu that had been placed on the table to check out what the chef was presenting them for dessert. It was more a force of habit than genuine interest.

As Simon was putting the menu back in its place, Jason suddenly stood up and strode off. Simon glanced over at Susan's flushed face. She just rolled her eyes. Simon turned back to the room in time to see Emily re-enter. She had obviously gone to the restroom herself. The vague memory of her voice this afternoon surfaced from the back of his mind. She had said they were synchronized for the day. She and Jason crossed paths midway. After a brief exchange of pleasantries, the two shook hands and Jason left the room with a satisfied look on his face but, the minute Jason had passed her and could no longer see her face, Emily allowed herself to grin broadly for a fraction of a second before composing herself back into the slightly amused expression Simon had noticed earlier.

Emily sat down prepared to turn her entire attention over to Susan. Instinctively, she liked Susan, and from a professional point of view she could really appreciate the work that had gone into the preparation of the summit. Emily gracefully slid into her seat and was just about to ask Susan a question when she felt the arrival of a presence in the chair on her left. She turned to look at the newcomer and was very surprised to see Simon Russell sliding into the unoccupied seat.

"I hope the two of you don't mind the intrusion, but it looks as though I've been deserted for dessert."

Susan ignored the very poor attempt at a pun. "Not at all. Emily, I'm not sure you know Simon Russell. Simon is one of our key speakers at this year's conference. Simon Russell, Emily White."

Emily's smile was dazzling as she proffered her hand toward Simon. "Actually, we've already met." Emily turned slightly toward Susan. "I have to admit I'm surprised. This morning, Mr. Russell was under the distinct impression that I have a problem with men." Her smile widened as she turned back toward Simon, who by this time had extended his hand to take hers. "You're very courageous to face the lioness in her lair, particularly since there are two of us." Emily was practically laughing at him.

Simon closed his hand over hers. Simon almost hesitated before closing his fingers around her hand. He hadn't realized she was so dainty. Simon was tall, but he wasn't a big man and he didn't have enormous hands, and yet, in comparison with Emily's delicate hand, he suddenly felt slightly awkward, like he was about to handle a very fragile porcelain vase. Emily's handshake was surprisingly solid. It was disconcerting. He liked the feeling of her hand in his and, for a split fraction of a second, he was reluctant to let go. He attributed it to the wine.

"I'm actually here to make amends. Truthfully, you said something at lunchtime today that I can't seem to get out of my head."

Emily raised her eyebrows inquisitively, waiting for Simon to continue.

"Your comment about wondering whether or not the problem had been formulated correctly. It really is an interesting point."

Emily smiled softly and sincerely, the way a mother smiles at her child. "Developing women's economic role in society is such a complicated issue. It's virtually impossible to separate the economic development from the cultural awareness and the perception of women in any given society. I don't think there is one generic approach or solution. There probably isn't even a nationwide approach. I think the problem probably has to be examined and addressed community by community, and in some cases almost person by person, based on the history of that particular community or individual. It's very hard to condense all of the factors that have to be taken into consideration into a two-hour roundtable discussion. I wasn't being fair today. I do think the discussion would have been more stimulating had there been experts from more than one field. I'm sure there is probably quite a bit of lateral discussion that goes on between all of the various organizations that deal with women's issues across the globe, and it would have been interesting to hear all of the different angles on the problem."

For the following hour, Simon and Emily discussed policy, politics, and culture. Simon did most of the talking. Emily was a good listener. Her questions, when she asked them, were astute and stimulating. Some were not easily answered and required a bit of thought, which was a challenge for Simon after three glasses of wine, although as he got caught up in the conversation, his head cleared.

Susan had participated in the first few minutes of the conversation but had then given up. Her mind drifted back to when she and Simon were first married. In the beginning, she had been enthusiastic about his work on various policy committees, but that was all they ever seemed to talk about and she was soon bored. Had they been able to spend more time together, Susan was sure she would have asked for a divorce earlier. As it was, the marriage had dragged on for fifteen years. It took a career change for her to see that she had been wasting her life on a nonexistent relationship, nonexistent because she had stopped caring years before.

Susan brought her mind back to the present. Emily and Simon were still deep in conversation.

She cleared her throat. "I wouldn't mind moving this conversation out onto the patio. It's a lovely night, and I think we could have our after-dinner drinks and coffee served there."

Emily smiled. "I should probably turn in. It's getting late." She rose as she spoke.

Simon and Susan had risen, too.

"Not before you try the cordial. It's a traditional local drink, and it's absolutely out of this world. Besides, it's already been paid for," Susan insisted.

"I'm not really much of a drinker."

Simon, who had been thoroughly enjoying himself, added, "It's not very strong. It's only a little after eleven; even Cinderella made it until midnight."

Emily laughed. "She was a lot younger than I am."

She would have left then, but Susan insisted and, since Emily felt guilty that she wouldn't be sponsoring next year's event, she agreed to join them on the patio for their after-dinner drinks. Susan went to tell the waiter at the bar while Simon and Emily moved out onto the patio.

The patio was empty. Simon indicated a table near the sliding glass doors of the restaurant, but Emily glided toward a table near the railing overlooking the city. She didn't feel like sitting down immediately. There was a gentle breeze blowing up from the city and Istanbul was spread out beneath them. Emily closed her eyes briefly, trying to capture something of the flavor of the city, a noise or a smell, but it felt like any other terrace in any other part of the world.

She sighed.

Simon, who had come to lean against the rail next to her, thought he understood her mood. "It's hard to believe we're at one of the gateways to the Orient. Istanbul has changed so much in the past fifteen years."

Emily turned to look at him. "It's the same in Beijing. The downside of globalization. I was in Hanoi last spring, and it's happening there, too, at a slower pace, but it's happening. Soon, no matter where you go, it's all going to be the same. It will be boring. When I think of how much has changed even in Italy in the twenty years that I've been there it depresses me. Shopping centers and franchises are cropping up everywhere. That's the problem with economic development. It's being implemented as a carbon copy of the U.S. Why bother developing local schools of architecture or art or literature or even music? Some of it probably should disappear, like South African horn blowing or Sardinian folk songs that sound like bleating goats, but it would be nice if something were to remain. The exchanges between cultures are what triggered the Renaissance. I really feel like we're living in a second Middle Ages. That we've crushed creativity and the world is slowly becoming a monotone gray." Emily felt herself blushing.

Simon stared down at her intensely. He couldn't remember the last time he had seen a woman blush, and it was oddly appealing. He was speculating on what else might make Emily blush when Susan, accompanied by the waiter, joined them with a tray and three small glasses shaped like miniature flutes. The three remained standing there, drinks in hand, quietly chatting about inconsequentialities until Susan's phone rang. Susan looked at the caller display. It was Richard. She smiled, took the call, and, gesticulating to her companions that she would return in a few minutes, walked back into the restaurant.

Neither one of them was really sure how it happened. Susan still hadn't come back and the two of them were just standing there chatting pleasantly. One minute, Emily was laughing at something Simon had said and he had innocently reached out to take her empty glass from her hand to set on the table behind her, but, on its way back from the table, his arm suddenly wrapped itself around her waist, pulling her toward him, and his lips met hers. There was nothing brusque in the movement. Everything had happened as fluidly as if they had been rehearsing for years, like two musicians playing the same note.

Emily gasped in surprise. Her parted lips were too much of an invitation for Simon's tongue. Simon's right hand moved to join his left hand and then, as his left hand slid upwards toward the nape of her neck, his right hand slid slowly down her back, urging her even closer to him. Emily went from shock to horror to fire in all of three seconds. She couldn't remember the last time she had been kissed like that. Truthfully, she didn't think she had ever been kissed like that. She tried to get her mind to dominate her senses but her body wasn't collaborating. She thought she heard herself moan as his tongue continued its gentle exploration of her mouth, wrapping itself around hers. She felt her arms go limp like she was drowning or losing consciousness. Her left hand grasped itself around the back of Simon's neck, her fingers trying to close around his short, cropped hair. Her right hand rolled lifelessly down his side, and the small clutch purse she had been jostling with all evening long fell silently to the ground as her body melted further into his. They both lost track of time. Simon's mouth moved from hers briefly to the hollow below her ear. The spasm of desire that wracked her body was so strong she felt certain she was going to collapse to the ground, dragging Simon with her. She tried to speak but Simon had traced his way along her jawbone back to her mouth where his tongue insisted on tangoing with hers again. The kiss deepened and then suddenly it wasn't enough. Simon's entire body went rigid with a jolt and he groaned in response to the ache that spread up from his groin across his body. He wanted more.

Up until that moment, there had been nothing premeditated in any of his actions. It had been an impulse of the moment driven by loneliness, hunger, an extra glass of wine, but now that he knew what he wanted, he was determined to get it. His breathing was ragged and his voice was husky with desire as he moved his mouth to her ear and whispered, "I want you."

The words made it through the fog that had wrapped itself around her brain. Emily went suddenly rigid and then broke free, taking a step back to look at Simon. She was literally shaking, her face a mask of mortification. Her breathing was so erratic she could barely speak.

"No…that shouldn't have…we…I…" She couldn't get a coherent sentence out. She took a deep breath and managed to expel the words, "I'm married."

Simon was silent, letting her speak. Like a predator with its prey, he let her think she could get away. The intensity of his expression sent another wave of heat throughout the lower part of her body.

Emily gasped, "I have to go."

She practically fled across the patio. Simon smiled to himself and then bent down to pick up her purse. He had felt it hit his foot when she dropped it. He then strode thoughtfully across the patio, wove his way through the tables in the restaurant out to where Emily was still waiting, in a high state of agitation, for the elevator to reach the top floor. He didn't say a word as he handed Emily her purse. Her eyes flew to his face. Something in the way she moved and looked reminded him of a caged bird desperate to take flight.

The elevator arrived and they both stepped in. Emily had been tempted to ask him to go on ahead but Simon was being very circumspect. He held the door for her until she entered. Emily pushed the button for the eighth floor. As the doors to the elevator closed, Simon reached across and pushed the button for the eleventh floor. The restaurant was on the eighteenth floor.

Emily clutched her handbag to her chest as if it were a shield. Simon's movements were slow and deliberate. He was so sure of victory that he was actually enjoying himself. As he moved in for the kill, his eyes never left her face. Emily stood mesmerized, her body still aching from his previous assault on her senses. She had her back pressed against the elevator wall by the control panel, facing Simon. He kept moving closer and closer until there was only a breath between them. His arms on either side of her blocked her movement and then he was kissing her again. He started with the hollow beneath her ear. Emily gasped, and the battle was lost without a fight.

When the elevator door opened, Simon was ready. With the ease of a ballroom dancer, he glided Emily out of the elevator, still kissing her until she was leaning gently against the opposite wall. His mouth firmly on hers, his left hand running havoc up and down her side, he pulled his key out of his pocket and opened the door. Why on earth had he been so annoyed at being placed in front of the elevators? The door opened with a click and then they were inside. Once inside, Simon gave free reign to his passion and Emily responded. It wasn't until his mouth cupped over her breast that she realized he had somehow removed her dress. She was in sensory overdrive, oblivious to everything except the waves of pleasure that were causing her to gasp and groan. Her body trembled at his touch, trying desperately to get closer. When he came inside of her it was like an explosion; a small cry escaped her and she crushed her lips against him to keep from crying out again. Simon tried not to increase his tempo, but three months of abstinence and Emily's responsive body beneath him were driving him totally out of control.

They both hit their climax together. Neither one of them was in control of their bodies at that point. They had both resorted to various primordial guttural sounds to express the pleasure they were experiencing, abandoning themselves to instincts that were older than time. When it was over, it took them both a long time to resurface and even then neither one of them had any desire to speak.

Simon shifted his weight so that he was lying alongside Emily, his leg still intertwined with hers. He pulled himself up onto his elbow so that he could look at her. His left hand continued a lazy inspection of her body. Emily turned her body toward his, still enjoying the feel of his skin against hers. She tried to make out the features of his face but it was impossible. She had lost her glasses at some point and she was as blind as a bat without them. She reached her right hand tentatively to trace the contours of his face. He took her hand in his and pressed it against his cheek and then turned to kiss her palm. Emily felt her body responding to his touch.

"Now what?" Her voice was so soft, it was almost a caress, and Simon was suddenly overcome with an emotion he couldn't describe, something between elation and awe. He let go of her hand to trace his hand down her arm, stopping when it got to her shoulder. He shifted his weight again so that he was almost on top of her and lowered himself until his face was just inches from hers before he spoke, his eyes never wavering. "I want to make love to you again. Only this time…" He kissed her gently, "I want to take my time."

And to make sure she understood what he meant, he brushed his lips softly against hers, his tongue pushing gently on her bottom lip, inviting her to open her mouth, and when she did, he kissed her, slowly and deliberately. For a long time after that, neither one of them spoke.

Morning had to come inevitably. Emily and Simon had spent most of the night making love and talking timidly the way that only newfound lovers can. They had talked about the morning, too. That had been right before they drifted to sleep. Emily had started crying. The realization of what she had done had finally caught up with her.

Until that evening, she had always thought she had values. In over twenty years of marriage, she had never once looked at another man, let alone contemplated the idea of having an affair. To make matters worse, making love with Simon had been better than anything she had ever experienced. How on earth was she supposed to go back to the mediocrity that was the best her husband had to offer? She kept this part of her thoughts to herself. She had wanted to leave then but Simon wouldn't let her go. He had pulled her to him, kissing her again, and they ended up making love for the third time that night. It was a much shorter experience than the other two, but after that, Emily lay on Simon's chest listening to his philosophy of carpe diem. When she had told him that she was afraid of what came next because she knew she wasn't the type for a one-night stand, he had held her tightly and said half-jokingly that he was counting on two nights. Emily kept quiet after that and they both fell asleep.

Simon woke up in the morning, Emily still nestled snugly against his side, with his arm around her. That surprised him because it was the first time since his marriage with Susan that that had happened. He usually woke up flat on his stomach at the far edge of the bed. The second thing that struck him was how wonderful he felt. It wasn't just a question of having quenched his sexual appetite. The sex had been fantastic. There were no doubts about their compatibility in that department—three times in one night. He hated to admit it, but he felt like a stud. He went back over the events of the night starting from the minute he had decided to join Susan and Emily at the table and that was when it hit him. He hadn't been bored.

After his divorce with Susan, Simon had tried dating. The women he picked up usually fell into one of two categories—dumb and pretty, i.e. very young, or intellectuals. The young ones had been fun to play with, and the smart ones had been fun to talk with, but he hadn't met anyone with the right equilibrium. Physically, most had been carbon copies of Susan. He had broken out of that routine with the one-nighters. He thought back briefly on those, six in all, seven including Emily. The first time, fifteen months ago, Clarice had done all the work. He had merely gone with the flow. Clarice had been married, too, but had made it abundantly clear that she didn't have any qualms about a little side action. After that, he had decided to take the lead. He didn't like pushy women. It had taken a little practice but by number six he had become a fairly smooth player.

Simon felt a thrill rush through him as he remembered the way Emily had melted in his arms. Emily stirred beside him. Simon looked down at her and sighed. Attractive and intelligent and…married, with three children. At that moment, Emily opened her eyes and Simon decided he wasn't going to analyze his behavior anymore. He wanted to enjoy the moment while it lasted.

When Emily slipped out of his room an hour later, it was still early morning. They had agreed to meet for breakfast at 8:45. The session on sustainable development started at 10:00. Emily felt extremely guilty as she stole out of Simon's room. Luckily, she didn't run into anyone on her way down to her room. She didn't know how she would have dealt with that. Her legs were shaking by the time she reached her door.

Inside the safety of her room, she collapsed on the bed. She could feel the tears coming. She was too emotionally strained to sob so she simply let them flow silently down her face onto the bed. She didn't know how long she lay there—her mind had gone blank—but the events of last night weren't going to be ignored. They insinuated themselves back into her brain. Emily found herself going over every aspect of their conversation at the dinner table and then outside on the patio. She honestly couldn't even remember what he had said to make her laugh. He had taken her glass out of her hand and then... She still felt the full force of their lovemaking. She could feel Simon in every fiber of her being. Just thinking about it made her pulse accelerate. She wanted desperately to be in his arms again. With a herculean effort, Emily threw herself off the bed and headed to the bathroom for a shower, hoping the water would wash away her sins or at least restore some sense of normality.

Emily stood under the hot water of the shower for over half an hour. By the time she turned the water off, she had broken the situation down into rational elements that she could deal with. The first was that sexual intercourse with Simon Russell had been the most incredible experience of her life and that if she had to burn in hell for all of eternity as a result, it had at least been worthwhile. The second was that if she wanted to avoid a repeat performance tonight, all she had to do was avoid him. When she had said as much to him last night he had threatened to do a "Hey Stella!" routine at her door, but she doubted that he would go through with it. He had a reputation to maintain, too. Everyone was entitled to a moment of weakness at least once in life. To give in again would be almost hedonistic. Third, she and her husband had been having problems with their relationship for over a year now, and she thought she might be able to put off having sex with him for a few months at least in order to give herself time to brace herself psychologically for the comparison. All things considered, she thought that was going to be the really tricky part.

Ignoring Simon Russell was virtually impossible. Emily got lucky at breakfast. Jason Hopper and Susan were at the buffet when she walked into the room and, mistakenly thinking that she was looking for a place to sit, had insisted on her joining them. Simon walked in a few moments later. If he was upset to find her already seated with other people, he didn't let it show. In fact, he looked like a man who had just won the gold medal in the decathlon. It only took him a few moments to invite himself to their table, moving the flowers and table decorations to make room for a plate, and pull up a chair. Sitting across from him at the table pretending that nothing had happened between them was torture. Simon was obviously more experienced and chatted pleasantly with Susan while Emily tried to smile at Jason's attempts to be charming. She was having a very hard time concentrating on what he was saying because part of her was listening to the conversation between Simon and Susan. They seemed to be intimately acquainted. Emily wondered how intimately. Susan had picked up on Simon's good mood and was apparently surprised by the quantity of food he was having for breakfast. Simon replied to her banter good-naturedly with innuendoes about burning calories and keeping his strength up that were obviously meant for Emily. Emily found herself blushing despite herself. She ate quietly and mechanically, contributing very little to the conversation, excusing herself as soon as was acceptably possible to return to her room. Simon rode up with her in the elevator, but because they were not alone, he limited himself to a quick caress down her back when he thought the others weren't looking.

Simon's schedule that day was light. He was chairing a policy debate at 2:30, but other than that he was free for the morning, and since he didn't feel like working, he decided to sit in on the Sustainable Development session. Emily was surprised to see him walk into the room. He had said he would be working on a report he had to turn in. He smiled at her and took a seat at the back of the room. Emily turned back to her notes.

The Sustainable Development session was structured as a roundtable discussion on policy, similar to the session Simon would be chairing in the afternoon. It was a moment for policy makers and industrial experts to compare notes and identify common strategies, areas for improvement, and collaboration between the public and private sectors.

Jason Hopper took his place. As moderator, his job was to keep the conversation flowing so that everyone had a chance to contribute his or her two cents' worth to the conversation. It was a two-hour discussion.

Thirty minutes into the debate, Simon was spellbound. Emily White wasn't only knowledgeable, she was also a natural leader. She had quietly taken over the table and was piloting the discussion with skill and dexterity. She cut through verbose presentations, getting to the core of issues, exposing underlying flaws in logic and structure in such a simple matter-of-fact manner that no one got angry. After forty-five minutes, she had gotten everyone to agree on their objectives in being there and the take-away from the session, and for the last hour she worked systematically to fill in the blanks and get everyone on board. In the last ten minutes, she was able to summarize everything they had accomplished, all the points that they had agreed upon, and all of the pending points that still remained to be addressed, and, more importantly, she had carried her point about the need to introduce life cycle assessment tools at all levels both in private and in public. In fifteen years of service, Simon had rarely seen anyone manage a meeting as effectively. He was blown away. He also felt a very irrational surge of pride. It reminded him vaguely of a conversation two colleagues once had about what kind of cars they had driven. Both had agreed that Italian cars were the best, but whereas the one colleague had only ever driven an Alfa Romeo, the other owned a Maserati.

Simon wasn't the only one who had been blown away by Emily White. After the debate, she was literally surrounded by men still interested in continuing the discussion. Emily nodded and smiled and listened politely, granting audience for a suitable amount of time and then courteously moving on to the next person. The empress and her court, Simon thought.

When the last of the dawdlers had taken his leave, Simon was standing there ready to take his place. "That was impressive."

Emily smiled shyly and shrugged her shoulders slightly. "It's a topic I feel strongly about."

"That was obvious. Lunch?"

Emily nodded. As she went to step forward, he put his hand on the small of her back and bent down to whisper, "It's taking every ounce of willpower I have not to drag you caveman-style to some dark corner to ravish you."

Emily trembled, and Simon grinned broadly as he piloted her out of the room, his hand pressing lightly against the small of her back. He dropped his hand as they moved out into the hallway. There were too many people mulling about.

Simon preceded Emily into the ballroom and was scooped up almost immediately by one of his fellow speakers, who wanted to hash through some ideas for their afternoon session. Emily continued to the buffet, staring blankly at the mass of food, but nothing appealed to her.

She took a small helping of couscous and vegetables and was making her way to a table in the corner when Susan intercepted her. "Emily! You have no idea. Everyone is raving about your session. I have had so many compliments. Everyone says you were fundamental to the discussion today. We may have to think about signing you on board as an official speaker. I don't know how to thank you enough. Thank you. Thank you. Thank you."

And then like a whirlwind she was gone. Emily smiled and shook her head slightly. She wasn't used to such enthusiastic praise. As she focused on the table she had been heading toward, it was suddenly taken. She glanced around the room looking for another corner to hide in. Simon was deep in conversation at the other end of the hall. Susan had just joined him, throwing herself under his arm. He laughed down at her and then grabbed her around her waist, tickling her and pulling her into an affectionate hug, kissing the top of her head.

Suddenly Emily felt nauseous; all of the color drained from her face. Turning on her heels, she dropped her plate on the nearest cocktail table and fled.

Simon looked up in time to catch the expression on her face and watched as she raced out of the room. It only took him a fraction of a second to realize that his exaggerated display of affection was to blame. Damn.

He pulled free of Susan, grabbing her arms, his face suddenly tense and serious. "Suz, I need a big favor. Call me at 2:25, and if I don't answer the phone, stall for me or fill in. Something urgent has just come up. I'll explain later."

Without even waiting for her answer, and a quick "Catch you later" to the other man, Simon headed toward the door. Emily was nowhere in sight. Damn. He pushed the elevator button aggressively. He kept pushing the elevator button. Last night, the fact that the elevator was so slow had worked to his advantage. Now it was driving him insane. The door opened. Simon had to wait for some guests to step off. He pushed the number eight, grateful he had remembered to ask her room number, 822. The doors took an eternity to close. The ride to the eighth floor seemed interminable. He wanted to squeeze his way through the doors as they opened but he wasn't alone. He was actually shaking. What on earth was he doing? He wasn't sure.

He knocked on her door. "Emily. Emily! I know you're in there. Open the door. We need to talk." And then he raised his voice. "I'm not afraid to shout!" He really hadn't meant to raise his voice that high, but panic had set in.

He heard a movement on the other side of the door. Emily opened the door and Simon burst into the room, dragging Emily with him. They were on the bed in a second. Simon was on fire, totally out of control. One hand found its way under her clothes to the smooth surface of her skin, the other wrapped itself around to the nape of her neck; his lips were everywhere, tracing circles from the hollow under her ear first on one side then on the other to her forehead, down her nose and then finally onto her mouth. He pressed his groin against her so that she could feel his hardness. Somehow his hand made its way into the soft folds of her vagina and Emily surrendered.

They were still fondling each other in the aftermath of their lovemaking when Simon's phone rang.

Simon sighed. "That will be Susan."

Emily stiffened beside him. Simon flipped himself on top of her so that he could look her in the eyes. "Emily. Susan is my ex-wife. We've been divorced for over five years now. We were married for fifteen years. She's a good friend but that's all there is. There definitely isn't any of this."

He swooped down to kiss her and would have kept on kissing her if the phone hadn't persisted. Simon groaned in protest and began looking for his phone. It was in the pocket of his jacket, which was in a crumpled heap at the bottom of the bed. "Yullo. Hi, Suz."

Simon turned to look at Emily and bent down to silently kiss her as Susan continued her tirade. Emily couldn't make out the words but she could hear the agitation. She sat up.

"If you would give me a minute to get a word in edgewise…I'll be there. Give me five minutes. Tell everyone I got stuck on a conference call." Simon rolled his eyes. Susan was really on a roll. "Susan. If you don't let me get off this phone now, I won't make it down on time. I promise you. Five minutes and I'm there. I'll explain later. Bye. Five minutes."

Simon turned to look at Emily. They both sat in silence, staring into each other's eyes. Simon reached over and cupped Emily's chin in his hand. His voice was low and full of emotion. "If I were to tell you that this…that you…were the most incredible thing that has ever happened to me in my whole entire life, would you believe me?"

Emily nodded because she didn't trust herself to speak.

Simon sighed. "I have to go. I'm supposed to be chairing the final session." His thumb caressed her lips. "Promise me you'll still be here when I get back."

Emily caught her breath for a moment and then nodded numbly. Simon almost lost his resolve. He pulled away reluctantly and, with concentrated effort, rapidly threw his clothes on. His jacket was too crumpled to put on so he folded it across his arm.

He threw Emily a crooked smile and said, "I'll have to blame the heat." Emily smiled, and a small chuckle escaped through her lips. Simon was still making love to her in his head when the doors to the elevator opened and he stepped inside. He focused. The elevators were going to get part of the blame for his being late.

Meanwhile, Emily had thrown herself back onto the bed, trying to come to terms with her thoughts. Eternal damnation was looking more and more like a certainty. Ignoring Simon had been impossible. And she was never going to be able to enjoy her husband's embraces ever again. The anguish that thought provoked caused a pain so strong she had to bite her pillow to keep from crying out. It was almost four before she was able to drag herself out of her misery. She decided to take a quick shower and meet Simon downstairs. On her way down to the conference area, she text messaged her husband and the kids, inventing an excuse for not calling. She didn't think she'd have the courage to talk to them.

Simon saw Emily slide into the room and take a place next to Susan at the back of the room. The session had gone well despite the delay in getting started and the fact that his heart really wasn't in it, but suddenly he couldn't wrap it up quickly enough. In what felt like forever, but was really only ten minutes, Simon was able to close the meeting. Now all he had to do was get past Susan, who was still evidently peeved with him. He wondered what perverse quirk had made Emily take her place near Susan.

Emily hadn't noticed she was taking a seat next to Susan until it was too late. Susan had smiled at her and indicated that the seat was free, so she had no choice but to sit there. Now they were standing together chatting about the day's program. Dinner that evening was still courtesy of the summit, but it was a more informal affair. Susan was just asking Emily if she planned on having dinner in the restaurant when Simon joined them.

"Ladies. Well, Suz. what's the verdict? I actually thought this was one of the best sessions I've ever chaired. There was some good debate going there for awhile, and I think some of the observations that were made may actually make it into the policy papers."

Susan glared at him. "You are forgiven because you are still one of the most competent professionals I have in my repertoire, but if you ever even slightly hint at abandoning ship like that again and *at the last minute*... You still owe me an explanation."

"I don't think Ms. White is interested in hearing our little spat. I'll tell you later."

Emily raised an eyebrow and, suddenly feeling very impish, said, "Oh, don't be put out on my account. I was actually planning on going down to the lounge. It's too late for an espresso, but I wouldn't mind a cup of tea. I missed lunch." And before anyone could say anything, she turned and left.

If Simon hadn't seen the hint of amusement in her eyes, he would have panicked. She was going to pay for that little stunt later. At the

41

thought of the ways he was going to make her pay, he smiled, and Susan had a revelation. She gripped his arm and pulled him to a corner of the room, where she hissed, "Tell me you're not having an affair with Emily White!"

"I'm not hav…"

But she cut him off. "You are! I can see it in your face. How could you? She's married."

"So was Clarice…and Yolanda and…"

"Those were different. Your brain wasn't connected."

"Come again?"

"You know what I mean. Those were clearly just physical encounters. Emily White connects at the cerebral level. I could see that last night."

Simon was annoyed. He didn't want to admit that Susan was right. "Listen, Susan. Whatever happened, happens, or is going to happen between Emily White and me is our business. Okay. I don't want to talk about it, especially not with you. I don't pry into your private life with Richard. Speaking of the devil, wasn't he supposed to arrive this afternoon?"

"His plane landed twenty minutes ago. He should be here in an hour."

"Good. That way you won't miss us at your dinner tonight. For the record, Jeffrey has invited me to the embassy tonight for an informal dinner party. The invitation is for two and, yes, I plan on inviting Emily."

"God. You're introducing her to Jeffrey already? You only just met her. This is serious, isn't it? How on earth do you expect this to work out? She's going to be flying back to her husband and three children tomorrow."

"I said we weren't having this conversation. It's off limits."

"Simon." Susan took his arm softly. "I was your wife for fifteen years. I know you and I care. I want you to be happy. To find someone you can grow old with. Emily White is fantastic but she's already taken."

Simon shook her arm off and strode away. "Bye, Suz." He hated it when she said she cared. Why did she ask for the divorce if she still cared? Not that it mattered. It was finally his turn not to care.

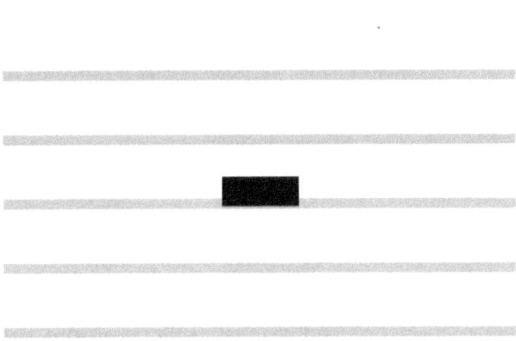

Emily was sitting at a table in a corner of the lounge, a pot of tea and a small plate of finger sandwiches in front of her. Simon could feel the tension leaving his body as he made his way toward her. "Mind if I join you?"

Emily laughed self-consciously. "I think you already have."

If she hadn't blushed, he would have missed the attempted innuendo.

He grinned, dropping his frame into the chair in front of her, and picked up a sandwich. "I missed lunch. How's the tea?"

"Hot."

The waiter came over, and Simon ordered a glass of iced tea. When he left, Simon cautiously approached the subject of how he hoped to spend the rest of the afternoon and evening. It was 5:00. Dinner at the embassy was scheduled to start at 8:30. Simon proposed a walk around downtown Istanbul until 7:00, when they could come back to the hotel and prepare for dinner at the embassy. Emily agreed to the walk around town, but she was harder to convince on the embassy dinner. They were still talking about it when they got back from their walk, but Simon wasn't taking no for an answer, which was why at 8:20, Emily found herself sitting next to Simon in a taxi on her way to the embassy.

Jeffrey Kinkade was an attaché at the embassy. He was short and balding and incredibly witty. He was also Simon's closest friend. The two men got together whenever they could, and Jeff was the only person Simon ever texted on a regular basis. They had met as interns at the World Development Bank shortly after college. They had both been posted in Istanbul. Simon had spent five years in Istanbul, leaving only when he married Susan. Jeff had married a native and had landed his job at the embassy eight years ago. He had a very good relationship with the current ambassador and his wife, and they were frequently organizing informal dinner parties with carefully selected guests. It was the best way to network and discuss policy without the formalities of court, as Jeff liked to say.

The guest list was relatively small—the ambassador and his wife, Jeff and his wife, the French ambassador and his wife, a Russian émigré, the heads of two of the most important banks in Istanbul with their respective spouses, and Simon with Emily. Simon and Emily were the first to arrive. Jeffrey was waiting for them in the vestibule. He started to make one of his usual comments, but his eye fell on Emily's wedding band, and he thought better of it. He greeted her politely with unveiled curiosity and cordiality. Simon could have shown up with any woman on the planet, even one with three legs and a beard, and Jeff would have treated her in the same affable manner. He genuinely adored Simon. Within ten minutes, Emily was thoroughly enjoying herself and felt as though she had known Jeffrey for years. As the other guests came in, Jeffrey handled the introductions. Emily spoke perfect French and was able to converse with the ambassador in his native language. She even managed to use the only Russian she knew, asking his wife, "How are you?" and then telling her, "I'm terribly sorry. I don't speak Russian."

She had a good ear for languages, and her pronunciation was good. The two women immediately hit it off and began exchanging experiences of places they had been, particularly in Italy. The Turkish bankers were interested in meeting Simon, and the crowd spontaneously divided into two groups that chatted pleasantly until dinner was served. Jeffrey kept the conversation flowing at dinner. He was basically a one-man show, laughing and joking with everyone.

The evening passed quickly. After dinner, the group moved back into the parlor, where coffee and cordials were served. Emily noted that it was the same as the one they had served the night before at the hotel. The group had separated again. This time the men were on one side of the room, discussing work, and the women were seated at the other, discussing life in general. As the conversation between the Turkish bankers and the ambassadors picked up, Jeff was able to pull Simon aside for a brief chat.

"So what's the scoop?"

"No scoop. Just a date for the evening."

"Yeah, right, and my left foot is a puppy. I've been watching you all evening long. Every time she opens her mouth, you look like you've just won the lottery, and you've been eating her with your eyes all evening long."

"Whoa. You're getting as bad as Susan. Emily and I met at the conference. She's a great lady but she's married and she's got three children that she's flying home to tomorrow."

"Well, she must have been good in bed for her to get that kind of a reaction out of you."

"Jeff, it's not…"

"Right…and my other foot is a kitten."

"You're impossible."

"We'll see."

"What's that supposed to mean?"

"You're the smart one. You figure it out." Their conversation was interrupted by the French ambassador, who wanted Simon's opinion on the point of fiscal policy they had been discussing.

Half an hour later, the conversation began to run down. The guests took their leave. Simon helped Emily into the waiting taxi and climbed in beside her. The ride back to the hotel was silent, each lost in his or her own thoughts. Inside the elevator, Emily went to push the button for the eighth floor, but Simon stopped her; holding her hand in his, he pushed the number eleven and the door close button. The elevator doors closed and they were alone. Simon's lips found hers and they repeated the scene from the previous night.

Morning came too quickly. It was over. Emily was the first to wake up. She lay there silently memorizing the feel of Simon's arms around her. She wondered if she would be able to call that memory up the next time she was making love with her husband. Would it help her get through the act or throw her into a state of deep depression?

Suddenly, she wanted to go back to her own room. How was she supposed to say goodbye? What did you say to someone you were probably never going to see again? Thank you and have a nice life? What had happened between them? *Just sex,* her mind shouted. *Just sex, just sex, just sex,* she repeated to herself. Then why did it feel like something more? Why did she want it to be something more? How was she going to face her husband? Emily lay in torment for over an hour until Simon opened his eyes.

The rest of the morning passed in a surreal blur. As Emily sat staring vacantly out the airplane window, she tried to remember what they had said to each other, but her mind stubbornly refused to go over the scene. She couldn't even remember packing. As the plane banked over the city of Istanbul, Emily felt the tears she had been trying to repress trickle silently down her face.

Andante un poco adagio

Emily arrived in Europe as an English language assistant fresh out of college. When her plane landed at London's Heathrow airport, she still felt as if she were dreaming. She had a week before her training program in Nice began, and she was going to spend it with her best friend, Mary, in London. Mary was on a year-long exchange program and was living in a student apartment near Piccadilly Circus. Mary had only been in London for six weeks and classes had started so she already had a full schedule, but that didn't stop the girls from making elaborate plans for their time together. They were going to explore every nook and cranny of the city.

Emily had already made her plans for the mornings while Mary was in classes, including two side trips to Stonehenge and Canterbury. She was going to have to watch her money. The exchange rate was awful. Everything was expensive, and she wouldn't receive her first paycheck until the end of September. She had spent the entire summer working two jobs and eating nothing but beans and rice, but her savings weren't going to get her very far.

Her parents had stopped giving her money when she left home to go to college, and she had been fending for herself ever since. Her dad had point-blank said that college was a waste of money because she was just going to get married and start a family. Her mother had simply given her a quick hug in one of her sober moments and said, "I'm sorry." They hadn't really spoken since.

And yet, here she was. In London! Her immediate future very clear before her. She would have an entire year in France to think about what she wanted to be when she grew up and where she wanted to live when she went back to the States. She couldn't believe her luck! She had been hoping for an assignment in Paris when she applied for the position, so the letter informing her that she would be spending the year in Antibes was a bit of a disappointment. Emily didn't know anything about Antibes except that it was on the French Riviera not too far from Cannes, but everyone she spoke to thought she was the luckiest person in the world, and she was beginning to think so herself.

It was a perfect week in London. The weather collaborated most of the time. It conveniently rained while they were in Portobello Road, giving Emily the excuse she needed to run into a secondhand clothing store and buy a genuine trench coat. She walked out of the shop sporting a full-length black number like a native Londoner.

Stonehenge was a disappointment. When she got off the bus, she found that the area was fenced off by an extremely high metallic fence. The entrance fee was too exorbitant for her meager budget, and it would have only taken her a few hundred feet further to where a second internal fence roped off the entire stone area. It wasn't at all in keeping with her fantasy of walking in the footsteps of some druid priestess, so Emily spent the rest of the morning perched on a road marker, waiting for the bus that would take her back to London. It was a whole new luxury to have nothing to do but sit and write in her diary. Her mind was finally free to roam at random with no particular care or worry. It was so intoxicating that her mind went blank and she doodled.

The whole week was intoxicating. Emily had never experienced true freedom before. She had always been too busy with the task of day-to-day survival. Years later, she would never be able describe in any detail what she had done that week; she had been like one of Plato's prisoners released from the cave; but London would always hold a special place in her heart as a result of that first giddy taste of liberty.

The week passed quickly as did the weeks that followed. It was December before she realized that life was beginning to fall into a routine and that she still hadn't given a minute's thought to her future. Christmas vacation was a more immediate problem. There were four language assistants in Antibes—German, Italian, and two English. The other language assistants were all planning on heading home for the Christmas holidays. Emily didn't have the money to fly back to the States, and she didn't know where she would go even if she did. The thought of seeing her mother and father for the holidays made her physically ill, anyway, so she was very grateful when the Italian language assistant, Claudia, invited her to spend Christmas with her family in Genoa. It was there, during a visit to Portofino, that Claudia made the suggestion that would define Emily's path in life.

That day in Portofino was exceptionally cold and damp, not at all the way Emily had imagined it would be. It was much colder than it had been in Antibes, but Portofino, without the cars and the crowds of summer, has a silent beauty that penetrates the skin. Emily felt the wind bite into her, heard the crash of the winter waves against the rock, and watched as the evening lights poked through the gentle fog that was rolling in as dusk fell. She and Claudia stood shivering at the top of the hill with their backs to the wind, mesmerized by the scene below them. Emily couldn't help but comment on how beautiful it all was. That was when Claudia suggested that Emily come to Italy to teach English after her contract in France expired. Emily didn't realize it at the time, but her decision was made before she even reached the bottom of the stairs that had taken them to the church and headed gingerly toward Claudia's parked car.

January through May passed in a heartbeat. Emily spent as much time as possible touring the coast, but most of her energy was spent in anticipation of her trip to Italy. It was still a trip at the time. She thought she'd spend a year at the most. The idea of going to a country where she didn't know anyone, didn't even know the language, without the certainty of even finding a job, caught her imagination and spoke to an inner need to prove herself that she hadn't even been fully aware existed. She knew as certainly as she knew her own name that this was something she had to do. She wanted to prove to herself that she was somebody.

It turned out to be much more difficult than she had imagined. It didn't help matters that she and Claudia had a falling out shortly after their return to Genoa. Claudia was extremely jealous of the way Emily had so effortlessly inserted herself into her circle of friends. She accused Emily of trying to steal her friends from her, and if it hadn't been for Antonella, Emily probably would have had to admit defeat. Antonella was part of Claudia's circle of friends, but the two girls did not really get along since they had both been interested in the same boy at one point in time. It was Antonella who found Emily her first teaching job and was instrumental in helping her find an apartment.

Unfortunately, even that friendship turned out to be short lived because Antonella's boyfriend Antonio started showing too much interest in Emily, helping her wade her way through all of the red tape to obtain a temporary stay permit. At that time, the only way to obtain a stay permit was as a tourist, so Emily had to leave the country every three months and come back in. She was being paid cash for her lessons, so technically speaking she was part of the black market. It was after her second trip across the border that Emily met Riccardo.

Riccardo was finishing his exams at the university and wanted to brush up on his English to prepare for the job interviews he knew were coming up. Even then, Riccardo had a very clear idea of what he wanted out of life. His father was a top manager in a large Italian multinational, and Riccardo planned on following in his father's footsteps. His father had already pulled strings to line up a series of interviews, including one with a very important international bank with offices in Milan. Riccardo was graduating in economics, and the banking position was exactly the type of job he wanted to obtain.

It would be a lie to say that it was love at first sight. Emily's self-esteem was so low that she couldn't even consider the possibility that someone might find her attractive. Riccardo, on the other hand, immediately saw the advantages of the match. She was pretty. She was intelligent, and she was American. Riccardo thought that might be useful in an international environment. Their children would be perfectly bilingual. Not that Riccardo was particularly interested in having children. It was just something he knew he had to do, a duty and obligation to his mother. Because he wasn't particularly enthralled by the idea of children, he could be objective about it.

Emily never even knew what hit her. They were married in early November, a little over a year after Emily's arrival in Italy. It was exceptionally quick by Italian standards but there were no significant obstacles to overcome. Riccardo's family owned several apartments in Genoa, two of which were vacant. Riccardo was hired at the bank in Milan even before his graduation ceremony. Emily had no one to express an opinion to one way or another. Her mother had pretended to cry when she phoned home to tell them the news, while her father stood in the background shouting obscenities and thanking his lucky stars that he hadn't paid her college tuition. They didn't come to the wedding.

Riccardo's father was unhappy with the match, but he was too much of a gentleman to let his feelings show. Riccardo's mother was an entirely different matter. With her, it genuinely was love at first sight.

She was sure her grandchildren would be breathtakingly beautiful. The only downside as far as the two women were concerned was the wedding ceremony itself. Emily was Catholic but Riccardo insisted he was atheist and refused to reconsider his position. At first, he had insisted that he wanted to get married in the town hall, but when his entire family opposed the idea, he agreed to a ceremony in the church. His position as an atheist meant that the couple had to get special permission from the church. It was a difficult negotiation with the parish priest, and he spent most of the wedding ceremony expounding the sins caused by a lack of faith rather than the joys and obligations of marital bliss. Riccardo's grandmother was so upset by her grandson's behavior that she refused to attend the wedding reception. It wasn't a very propitious beginning.

The early years of their marriage were probably pretty much the same as most marriages, where the husband is only interested in the convenience and the wife is so totally in love with the idea of being in love. Riccardo's father found Emily a job in the sales office at his firm. Emily genuinely enjoyed being regularly employed. She had a permanent stay permit and was finally becoming proficient enough in the language to take part in more complex conversations. Even

Riccardo's father had to admit that she was much smarter than he had originally thought and that his son could have done worse.

Riccardo, on the other hand, was too busy pursuing his career to give Emily much thought. They hadn't even been married a year when he took an apartment in Milan. The two-hour train ride back and forth between Milan and Genoa was just too much for him. Emily wasn't particularly thrilled with the idea, but she had grown up with far greater sacrifices and burdens and tended to take everything in its stride.

Meanwhile, work was providing its share of satisfactions. The new head of strategic marketing was looking for an assistant and someone suggested that Emily might be good for the job. After a two-hour interview, the manager decided that Emily was overqualified for the job and offered her a position on his staff.

Emily didn't know it at the time, but she had just taken her first step up the corporate ladder. It would be years before she took another step. As Emily was to discover, careers in Italy take time, and if you are a woman with any desire to have a family, they take four times as long. Still, it was recognition, and Emily quickly demonstrated that it was well deserved.

Riccardo was genuinely satisfied with his life. Emily was everything he had imagined in a wife. She always cooked his favorite foods, kept an impeccable house, and made him look good whenever they went out. They were never together long enough to have a serious fight, and the stability of their sex life was so reassuring that Riccardo could have gladly done with more, but he felt that that was the price he had to pay if he wanted to reach top management by the time he was thirty-five. He threw most of his drive into his ambition.

At thirty, Riccardo made his first career move. A major Italian bank from the Veneto region was expanding its international operations and was looking for a dynamic young manager to spearhead the operation. Riccardo applied for the job. He was so excited about his promotion that he forgot to take precautions, and that was how their first child, Benjamin, came into being. It was also the cause of the first real difference between the couple.

People get married for a lot of different reasons, some of which are probably inexplicable to those looking in from the outside.

Generally speaking, couples that marry for passion tend to find themselves in divorce court before year three. Emily had married Riccardo to start a family. That was the main purpose behind matrimony, particularly for those in the Catholic Church, and Emily considered herself Catholic. Riccardo had married Emily for the children, too. He just had an entirely different concept of family and the role he was supposed to play. Emily was slowly beginning to understand the difference in their points of view.

The idea that Emily was supposed to stay in Genoa while Riccardo moved to Veneto was entirely unacceptable to her, especially because he thought he would come home every fifteen days to avoid the stress of travel. Emily began hunting for a job in Veneto. It didn't go very well. She was pregnant, and no one wanted to take the risk. It would have been frustrating if she hadn't also been caught up in all of the preparations for the arrival of their son. Riccardo, hoping to appease her, promised her that it would be temporary.

Two years later, Emily had had enough of their temporary situation. She wanted her family to be together. She finally found a small company that made industrial electric motors for washing machines and other household appliances that was willing to take her on. She had returned to work after only the minimum three-month maternity leave, and her son was still young enough that no one expected her to have another child. It was a significant cut in pay and responsibilities, but that was a price Emily was willing to pay if it meant having a family her way.

Riccardo was actually touched that Emily would go through so much trouble to be with him and, since his mother seemed to think that Emily was doing the right thing, despite her constant complaining that her grandchild was being taken from her, he made the effort to find a house.

Shortly after they were settled in, Riccardo received a promotion. Their daughter, Erica, was born nine months later. It was during her pregnancy with Erica that Emily's fairy-tale vision of the world shattered.

The pregnancy with Erica was difficult. Emily almost had a miscarriage toward the end of her third month. The doctor prescribed that for the rest of her pregnancy, she stay flat on her back in bed. Riccardo did his best to lend a hand with Benjamin in the evenings but he did so grudgingly. For one thing, he was tired. He was putting in ten- to twelve-hour days because the bank was trying to establish services in the United States and, given the time difference, his work with his colleagues in the States didn't begin until mid-afternoon. He also felt slightly annoyed that his role as breadwinner wasn't being respected. Not only did he have to earn the bread, but he had to butter it, too. It didn't seem fair. Luckily, Riccardo's mother agreed to come and live with them until the baby was born. It took part of the edge off. Riccardo was now free to put in even longer hours at the office.

After Erica was born and her mother-in-law had left, Emily thought her life was complete. She was so focused on getting to know her daughter that she completely ignored Riccardo's late nights. She probably would have realized eventually that he was never around and then accepted it as a natural evolution in their relationship if it hadn't been for the phone call. It was early evening. As Emily was putting Erica into her bassinet, the phone rang. Since Riccardo still hadn't come in yet, she went into the master bedroom and picked up the phone thinking it was him. The woman at the other end of the line presented herself as Riccardo's lover and then proceeded to tell Emily what a selfish whore she was for refusing him a divorce. As the other woman's tirade rose to hysterics, Emily slammed down the phone. She was shaking so hard she could barely move. She was still sitting there rocking back and forth in a state of utter and complete shock when Riccardo walked in.

When she saw him in the doorway, her eyes grew wide, the pain spreading out of her chest and into her face.

"How could you!" It was the only thing she could think of to say and then she burst into tears.

The pandemonium that ensued woke the children up. Years later, Emily would try to conjure up the scene, but her mind refused to even go there. It was as if she had locked the memory behind an iron door and thrown away the key. Riccardo had cried, he had begged and pleaded her forgiveness. It had been a moment of weakness, nothing to compare with the feelings he had for Emily. She was the love of his life.

The mother of his children. When Emily locked herself in the bathroom to cry, Riccardo had called his mother. Riccardo's whole family got involved, reminding Emily that they had two small children to raise. How could she deprive them of their family? What option did she have but to forgive him? She had taken a significant cut in pay to move the family to Veneto. She certainly never would have been able to support the children on her own, and the idea of receiving alimony was anathema to her. She knew that if she were to leave Riccardo, she wanted a clean break. The family's constant barrage and these simple financial considerations worked. Emily caved in.

Family was important, especially to Emily, who had grown up in such a troubled home. How could she turn her back on so many caring people? Everyone had taken her side even as they were pleading Riccardo's case. How could she deprive the children of their chance to belong to this family? She began to convince herself that Riccardo was a good man despite this *moment of weakness*, as everyone was calling it. And, underneath it all, some small part of her felt that it was the Christian thing to do. She had tied her life to his for better or for worse. There was no turning back.

Riccardo was a model husband after that, at least by his standards. Another career change took him to a Paris-based international finance firm. Like with his previous promotions, he celebrated with Emily, and nine months later Toby was born. Emily had secretly hoped that Toby would be the glue that finally put their relationship back together, but it didn't work out that way.

Life rarely works the way you plan it. Shortly after Toby's birth, Emily's firm was purchased by an American multinational, and Emily was catapulted from her sleepy small-town marketing job to corporate. The next ten years would be a constant struggle juggling family commitments and growing responsibilities in the office with a husband who was almost always absent. When he was home, Riccardo did his best to help, but he was often tired and nervous. He had become a workaholic, his Blackberry a permanent extension of his body, and it's hard to hang out laundry or take out the garbage and text at the same time. So, although he was physically present with his family when he was in town and on the weekends, it always seemed to cost him a great deal of effort, and they all subconsciously breathed a sigh of relief when Monday rolled around and he had to take off again. Riccardo was in Paris Monday through Wednesday. Thursdays and Fridays he usually spent in the company's district office in Vicenza.

He and Emily went through the motions of being a family, but Emily knew deep down inside her that they really weren't. She did her best to hide it from the children and they actually grew up in fairly blissful ignorance.

Riccardo did little to hide his feelings. He resented the demands he felt the children placed on his existence and longed for the carefree days of their early married life. Riccardo overtly blamed the children for his lack of intimacy with his wife, never once questioning what he had ever done to deserve or develop an intimate relationship with her beyond asking her to marry him. The children, too young to understand the situation, just thought their father thought they were inadequate.

The fact that Riccardo thought his family obligations were a constant burden weighed on Emily enormously. Emily drew further and further away from her husband's steady state of unhappiness. Physically, they had virtually nothing in common, and their lovemaking was mechanical at best.

Emily turned to the church for support, becoming heavily involved in their local parish. As soon as they were old enough, she enrolled the children in Scouts. The four of them were all very active in their local community, and it was a source of pride and joy for Emily. She could live with being unhappy. She had been unhappy most of her life, had known worse experiences. If her children could grow up in a carefree environment—safe and healthy and happy—it was more than she thought she deserved. If only Riccardo were as accepting of his fate.

Emily embraced midlife with good grace. Inwardly, she cringed at the encroaching years, her declining eyesight, her first gray hairs. Outwardly, she always seemed to be laughing; even when she was serious, her eyes would sometimes twinkle in merriment at some inner thought or joke. Riccardo, on the other hand, felt the passing years were a cruel inside joke between Life and Death. His unhappiness increased.

When Simon got back from Istanbul, he tried to convince himself that he really was having a midlife crisis. Nothing made sense anymore. He threw himself vigorously into an intense work schedule to keep his mind occupied, but the past kept worming its way into his thoughts, especially when he walked into the emptiness of his flat late at night.

He forced himself to focus on the distant past, trying to identify how he had gotten to this point in his life. Simon was not the kind of person who dwelled on the past, but he needed the comfort of happier times to keep his mind from wandering to places he knew were off limits. Work was not helping.

Simon had met Susan at a bar in Istanbul. She and her friends were taking a Mediterranean cruise, and their ship was docked in the harbor for the night. They had taken a taxi into town and were sitting at a table at a very fashionable bar in one of the international hotels in downtown Istanbul. It was one of Simon and Jeffrey's favorite spots. Obviously, they noticed the young women as soon as they entered the place.

Jeffrey was already courting Fatima at the time, but he was a hopeless flirt and he really wanted to help his friend fall madly in love. As easygoing and extroverted as he was, it wasn't long before he and Simon were safely ensconced at the girls' table. Jeffrey was regaling them all with tales of his life in Istanbul, leaving Simon the opportunity to relax and chat with the very pretty strawberry blond on his left. Simon wasn't looking for a serious relationship at the time. He still had another year to go on his internship before he headed back to England to take up a real job.

Susan, on the other hand, was very much looking for a serious relationship and had set very high standards for herself. Simon seemed to fit the bill. His father was a retired diplomat, his mother a former BBC employee. He had connections and money. He was also obviously very intelligent and shyly ambitious. With the right woman behind him, he was sure to go far, and Susan was going to do everything in her powers to make sure that she was that woman.

It turned out to be easier than she thought. Simon's parents had married out of love and their marriage had been one of those very rare examples of what a marriage should be. Simon's father was attentive to a fault, always treating his wife as his better rather than his equal. In recompense, she treated him with even more respect. Simon was their only child, and they probably spoiled him a bit, but it was very natural for both of them to include him in their feelings for each other. Simon was very willing to fall in love. By the end of his internship in Istanbul,

Susan and Simon were engaged, and within a year of his return to England, they were married.

Susan encouraged Simon in his career choices, and she reveled in the privileges that his increasing success brought her but, as his career took off, he began spending more and more time away and Susan sadly discovered that she really didn't miss him. Simon's father had spent a great deal of time away from home when Simon was younger, so Simon thought it was perfectly natural that he should be away so often. He never realized the impact it was having on his relationship because it never occurred to him that Susan's feelings were different from his mother's. Not that he didn't know the two women were different. Susan, for example, didn't want children. She was a public relations manager for a small non-profit organization involved in women's rights development in third-world countries. It was Susan who had encouraged Simon to get involved in these issues, and when he landed a job at the Development Bank, she was thrilled. Simon mistook her enthusiasm for love. Susan thought Simon's new position would be beneficial to her non-profit, but Simon turned out to be strongly opposed to asking the bank to sponsor Susan's events because he didn't want to be accused of favoritism.

That was probably the beginning of her disinfatuation with Simon. As Simon moved into international consulting and policy, Susan became even less enchanted. Susan lost interest in her non-profit organization, too. She was tired of organizing events on a shoestring budget that were constantly losing money. She began looking around and finally found The Leadership Group. The Leadership Group was a consulting firm that had diversified into organizing forums, conventions, and seminars, putting together key figures from academia, industry, and government to stimulate dialogue between the three. It was also a very good way of making money to help offset eventual downturns in the consulting side of their business.

Richard Atkins, one of the senior advisors and partners of the firm, held the interview. He and Susan understood each other from the first moment. The names in the Group's repertoire of speakers were impressive, exactly the type of people Susan wanted to be dealing with. When she told Simon the news, he was genuinely excited for her. When she said that her career change entailed a divorce, his world caved in. He tried in vain to reason with her, to no avail.

When she actually moved out, he flew to Istanbul where he proceeded to get royally drunk with Jeffrey one evening, hoping that would somehow help, and then, more out of pride than anything else, he decided to accept her decision, going out of his way to show her that they could still be friends. And strangely enough, they were. They spoke just as often on the phone. They saw each other almost as frequently as they had before. The only thing that was missing from their relationship was the sex and, perhaps, some of the intimacy.

Whether Susan was acting out of guilt or she honestly thought that Simon would be an excellent speaker, she had included him in the first World Economic Development Summit. Simon had taken it as an invitation to rekindle their relationship, but Susan was already dating Richard Atkins and wasn't interested. Despite the awkwardness this caused, Simon was a huge success and the summit became a regular standing appointment between the two.

Thoughts about the summit brought his mind back to the subject he had been intentionally avoiding...Emily. His body missed hers. Just thinking about their nights together set his veins on fire. He did everything in his power to get her out of his system, but the loneliness of his bed at night had him quite literally writhing between the sheets. He actually woke up in a pool of his own semen after one particularly erotic dream. That was something that hadn't happened to him since he was a teenager.

It had been just over a week, and his desire seemed to be increasing rather than decreasing. He thought he was going to lose his mind. He had even gone as far as to call Susan and ask for the attendee list from the summit. It was definitely a midlife crisis...a crisis anyway...definitely a crisis. Simon did what he always did in a crisis; he called Jeff.

"I was beginning to think you'd given up on me. You do realize, of course, that I've sent you three perfectly good jokes this past week and all I've gotten back in return was one measly little smiley face." Jeff's sunny disposition burst across the ocean and hit Simon in the face. Maybe this hadn't been such a good idea.

"Just…been busy."

"Okay, cut the crap or my puppy's going to start scratching his tail. When you're too busy to drop me a line, you're either dating or depressed, and you sound like someone who's just discovered that all of his socks are pink."

Simon smiled despite himself. Jeff was always going to be Jeff. He tried to formulate his feelings but he couldn't seem to get the words out. The stress made his breathing erratic.

"It's just…I can't…I think…" was all he could manage between breaths.

Jeff gave a low whistle and was serious for a minute. "That bad, huh?"

"I don't know what's wrong with me. I can't seem to get her out of my head. During the day I seem to be able to focus, but at night…"

Jeff sniggered, "Doesn't sound like she's in your head, champ, unless your head is in front of your butt."

"In your case, that would be the same difference." Simon felt the tension slowly ebbing out of his body.

"Emily is not really the right kind of name for an enchantress, don't you think? It should be something more exotic like…" Jeff paused a second. "Do you know, I can't actually think of an exotic girl's name at the moment. I mean woman's name. Don't get me wrong, she made a very good first impression, but I really am having a hard time understanding where all of this pathos is coming from. This isn't your first time at bat. Of course, as you may recall, I saw this coming."

"You did, so now if you would kindly help me figure out where it's going."

"Get her out of your system. Move on."

"I'm trying."

"I don't know. What are your options? I'm assuming you've tried a cold shower?"

"Several."

"Go get laid."

"You're joking of course."

"No. You're single. No one is holding you down. Go pick up some delightful creature down at the pub or seduce an intern or…hump a colleague."

"I didn't realize you could be so crude."

"I'm trying to get you to see things in perspective. Your only other option is to call her. Tell her she was the best sex you've ever had and ask her if she'd be willing to repeat the experience, let's say, same time next year? Wouldn't that be smashing—you, Susan, and Emily. It almost sounds like a family reunion. There's just one tiny little problem with that. She's married, and it's not a life. You need a life."

"Thanks, Jeff, now I'm really depressed."

"Don't worry, I've got a puppy here that is itching to get at your backside and a kitten who's willing to scratch you anytime you need. Fatima wants to know what you're doing for Christmas." And with that, Jeff launched vigorously into a series of new topics. Jeff kept them both involved in lively frivolous banter for another quarter of an hour. Their conversation ended with Simon promising to spend Christmas together and Jeff promising to fly over for the weekend just as soon as he could make the arrangements.

As Simon started to put his phone back into his pocket, he felt himself slipping into a bottomless pit. What were his options? He gripped his Blackberry and rapidly scrolled down to Susan's email, opened the attachment, found the listing he was looking for, and hit speed dial. It was 6:30 p.m.

Emily was sitting at her desk in Milan when the phone rang. She always worked late when she was in Milan. It was better than sitting in a hotel room, and there was always plenty to do. At that particular moment, she was working on next year's budget. The new CFO, a young kid with a master's in finance from the Bocconi and very little experience, had convinced the CEO to change procedures.

The new spreadsheets were a nightmare, very complicated. Emily, who had gotten budgeting down to a fine science, was now struggling to match the voices in the current year's budget with the new cost structure. For example, were Magazine Subscriptions supposed to go under Advertising & Sponsorships or General Expenses? Not that the amount they spent on magazine subscriptions was significant, but Emily had never had this expense in the marketing budget before. Subscriptions were generally billed to the function that received and read the magazine.

She was so concentrated on the spreadsheets that she didn't even bother to look at the caller ID. She just assumed it was one of her children. When she recognized his voice, her heart started pounding violently in her chest, and she could feel a sense of panic rise up from the floor. She felt as though she were shaking like a leaf.

"Emily? This is Simon…Simon Russell."

Could he hear her heart pounding? "I…I can't speak…I'm busy," was the best she could stammer out. As she was hitting the disconnect button on her cell phone, she heard him say, "I'll call back."

Emily let the phone slide onto her desk and put her head between her hands. Her entire body went numb with shock. She wasn't even sure how long she sat there like that. Her brain slowly came back to life. For ten days, she had shut every single thought of Simon Russell out of her mind, concentrating on the mundane details of family life and escaping to Milan to avoid her husband.

The budgeting process always required extra work, and the new CFO had conveniently provided Emily with an excellent excuse to be in Milan more than was usual. It was hard on Toby, but the older kids were handling her absence well. A couple of times in her hotel room at night she had found herself slipping into unbidden thoughts but had always managed to force herself to think of the children and drift off to sleep.

As the neurons in her brain returned to normal speed, other sensations kicked in. Emily felt the heat invade her body. That got her moving. She closed the files she had been working on and turned off the computer. She would go to the hotel and use the gym; she could always work on budgets later. She knew it was going to be impossible to sleep. As she was waiting to disconnect her PC from its base, she looked at her cell phone. Her last call was from *numero sconosciuto*. Simon's number wasn't registered. Emily grabbed her PC and left the office.

Meanwhile, sitting alone in his London flat, Simon was starting to feel normal again. He had made his decision and he was over the first hurdle. He wasn't sure where any of this would lead him but he knew beyond a shadow of a doubt that he would be seeing Emily White again before the month was out. It was the only way he was going to get her out of his system, he told himself. He walked over to his desk and turned on his home computer. He needed to reorganize his schedule and check out flight information to Italy.

Emily was on pins and needles all the following day. Every time the phone rang, her stomach muscles tightened as if bracing for an impact. It was 5:00 p.m. when Simon called again.

"Pronto."

"Emily? Is now a good time to speak?"

"I…" Emily gasped. "I really don't…"

"Please. Look, just listen to me for ten seconds. That's all I ask. Don't hang up. I really need to see you again. I'm not asking to pick up where we left off. I'm not…I won't put any pressure on you but…" Simon took a deep breath. "I just really need to know that you were real. I need…I want…" at this his voice faltered. What could he say? I want us to be friends? I want to lock myself in a hotel room with you and never come out. I want to prove to myself that you were just a one-night stand?

"Simon." Emily was having trouble breathing. She had to grit her teeth to speak "I…don't think…that's…a good idea."

"I have to be in Italy next week," Simon lied. "I could fly into Venice. We could meet somewhere. Have coffee. Please say yes."

The minute Simon mentioned Venice, Emily practically hyperventilated. It was too close to home, her husband, the children. At the same time, the sound of his voice was sending her hormones into overdrive. She could feel herself losing control; it was too much stress.

"I'm sorry…I'm…I'm going to be in Milan all of next week." Before either of them could say anything else, she disconnected the call. Her hands were shaking so badly that she had to use both of them to turn the phone off. She had been planning on working until 7:00 p.m. to let the worst of the traffic out of Milan pass, but suddenly the traffic seemed totally irrelevant. As quickly as she could, she shut everything down and left the office. She didn't turn her phone back on until the following morning. She had three unreturned calls from *numero sconosciuto*.

For the first time in her life, Emily was grateful she had two offices. She had registered for the summit using her Veneto address. That was where she spent most of her time since it gave her a chance to be with the children, but there was no way she intended to be there at any time during that following week. What if Simon were to show up at her office? Just the thought brought butterflies to her stomach. She wasn't happy about leaving the kids again, but she wasn't in any condition to be much of a mother either, and she really did need to get her budgets done. It was something she knew she could have done perfectly well in Veneto but her factory was in a small town. She somehow felt safer in the anonymity of Milan.

Emily was so engrossed in the task of waiting for her taxi that she nearly jumped out of her skin when she felt someone tug gently on her arm, calling her name. She knew who it was even before she turned to look at him. Simon was tense. He tried to smile but his face was guarded.

"I had to see you again."

Emily was shaking; the sudden rush of adrenaline almost made her dizzy. As she stood there trying desperately to think of something to say, her taxi pulled up. "My taxi," was all she could lamely manage.

Simon's grip on her elbow tightened slightly as he pulled her off the curb. He passed her into the car and then slid in beside her, telling the driver, "Hotel Diana Majestic."

The driver repeated the name of the hotel and then busied himself with the traffic; the meter was already running. Simon continued to stare at Emily. He wanted to kiss her but he was suddenly very unsure of himself. He could feel the stress and tension emanating out of her body in physical waves. She looked as though she were on the verge of a nervous breakdown. He studied her face carefully. Emily couldn't take her eyes from his face either.

Finally Simon said softly, "You look tired."

"I…" She paused and then exhaled, "…haven't been sleeping well. How did you…?"

"Internet. I called this afternoon and asked what time you usually leave the office. I told them I had some papers to drop off."

Emily turned her face to look out the window. Simon reached over and cupped his hand around the base of her neck, pushing a strand of her hair back into place. Emily nearly crumpled at his touch. "Don't," she pleaded, closing her eyes against the onslaught of desire she felt coursing through her.

His hand slid down her arm. Emily's heartbeat increased. Simon's lips were just inches from hers when the taxi pulled to a stop in front of the Diana Majestic. Emily hadn't realized her office was so close to the hotel.

The Diana Majestic is one of the most prestigious hotels in Milan. During the summer and on weekends, the candlelit lounge and bar is full to overflowing with beautiful people from the fashion world. During the rest of the year, it's a very good place to go for a discreet drink. On that Tuesday night in October, the entrance hall was virtually empty. Emily didn't really know what they were going to do or, to be more honest, she was refusing to think about it. Simon led her silently to the elevators, putting his arm around her waist. The ride up to his floor was quick. Neither one of them spoke as Simon opened the door and led her into his room.

When the door closed behind her, Emily felt a sudden surge of panic and turned to face Simon, but he was standing too close. She heard him sigh her name as his body closed in on hers. It was exactly the way both of them remembered it. Until that moment, both of them had tried repeatedly to convince themselves that it wouldn't be, couldn't be, the same. Simon realized he had been lying to himself when he had told Jeffrey he was flying to Milan to get her out of his system. The pleasure he felt at that moment was like a drug.

Emily always considered the months that followed as one of the bleakest periods of her life. It was virtually impossible for the two of them to meet, given the logistics. Between mid-October and December, they met twice, six nights in all, including four blissful days in Amsterdam because Emily had decided to supervise her company's presence at a trade show and Simon was able to take time off. They spent increasingly longer hours on the phone, particularly whenever Emily was in Milan, trying desperately to juggle schedules and reveling in the sound of each other's voice.

Christmas was a nightmare. Emily could barely stand to be in the same room as her husband, but her offices were closed until after Epiphany. Emily felt like a car with four gears—guilt, longing, anger, and neutral. There was no room for a fifth gear, and she couldn't seem to find reverse. If it hadn't been for the presence of her children, she would have lost her sanity. They were the only reason she dragged herself out of bed every morning.

Under guise of the Christmas celebrations, Emily was able to spend long hours in church. Once it had been her only solace. Now she felt the eyes from the cross burning down upon her hypocrisy. She understood now that she had never been able to forgive her husband those many years ago when he had had his affair. She had let her resentment destroy their marriage. She hadn't remained by his side out of faith. It had been lack of opportunity. If only she had been able to forgive then. She forgave now even though she knew it was too late. Too late for all of them.

February brought an unexpected change. Simon was able to use his connections to obtain a six-week seminar at the Bocconi University. Emily invented a new project that required her in Milan on Thursdays and Fridays. She went down on Wednesday evening a couple of times and stayed one Friday night, claiming she was too tired to face the drive home. It wasn't enough. By the end of February, Simon was begging Emily to leave her husband.

Everyone at work knew something was wrong, but no one suspected Emily was having an affair. Externally, Emily looked drawn and tired. Internally, Emily was falling to pieces. It was mid-March. Simon had flown back to London early that Friday afternoon. Emily left Milan to head home before the evening rush hour began. Driving took her mind off of things; besides, the kids had asked her if she was coming home early for her birthday and she didn't want to disappoint them.

It was 7:30 when Emily walked through the door. The kids were there waiting for her.

"Surprise!"

Erica had made dinner. Ben had taken care of the cake, and Toby had used his allowance to buy her a necklace. He had also made her a flower using wood and scotch tape. Riccardo wasn't home yet. They waited half an hour for him to show up. They all took turns calling him on his cell phone, but he never answered. Finally Emily suggested they eat without him. Everyone was subdued. The party atmosphere had turned sour. It didn't help matters that dinner was practically cold. Erica wanted to put everyone's plates in the microwave but that would have ruined the pasta. She was furious and ate in stony silence, occasionally barking at her brothers for no apparent reason.

The cake revived their spirits a bit, but by 8:45, it was all over. Emily tried Riccardo again. Still no answer. She would have been worried if she had had the energy to think about it. The kids went to bed at 10:00. Emily was tired but she was also emotionally drained. She had finally hit rock bottom. She was forty-seven years old. Just a short step from fifty. She was so depressed that she had to sit down.

She was still sitting there in the dark when Riccardo walked in the door. It was 3:00 a.m. She could see his face in the light that came in from the streetlamp as he closed the door. He didn't look tired, he looked…satisfied. Emily almost laughed out loud at the absurdity of it all. Riccardo was having an affair.

Just as this realization was whizzing from brain cell to brain cell, Riccardo flipped on the lights and was startled to find himself face-to-face with the last person he expected to see. He watched as her newfound knowledge wrote itself across her face. His eyes grew suddenly cautious but, before he could open his mouth to speak, Emily took charge. She was careful to enunciate each word slowly, pausing as though she were uttering a magic spell: "I want…a…divorce." Bibbity…bobbity… boo.

Allegretto grazioso

The autumn breeze blew briskly around Emily as she stood on the street beneath her flat. It was hard for her to believe that more than six months had passed since her birthday. She shuddered at the thought. That night had to have been one of the worst nights of her life. She and Riccardo had had a terrible argument that ended in him actually hitting her. The force of his blow had sent her glasses flying, and she had lost her balance. Her face smashed against the corner of an antique solid oak table. Stunned, bleeding, and scared, she had scrambled into the kitchen to find a frying pan, groping her way through the rooms like a blind person. Without her glasses she couldn't see a thing. Riccardo had followed her horrified and suddenly meeker than a lamb. The sight of Emily's bloody face had shocked reason back into him. He tried to hand her her glasses, which had broken neatly in two. Emily cowered as he came toward her. The nightmare of her beatings as a child came rushing to the surface. She began crying and whimpering in anticipation of more pain. Riccardo, defeated, backed out of the room, leaving her to lick her wounds. Emily had remained crouched in the kitchen for over an hour and then cautiously made her way back into the living room to dig her phone out of her purse. She somehow made her way to the cellar, where she silently called Simon.

The weeks that followed had been a nightmare. Riccardo refused to move out of the house so Emily had been forced to find an apartment. Not an easy task in a small town. Simon flew over as soon as he was able. They met in Milan. Emily's face was still bruised, and he was shocked beyond belief. He tried to convince her to hop on the first plane to London but the children were still in school. Emily wasn't budging until June. Riccardo hounded her incessantly. The children were angry and upset. Emily felt like an empty shell.

Simon had taken care of everything. Through connections, he met with the divorce lawyer and oversaw all of the paperwork, even though it was in Italian. All Emily had to do was sign. He arranged their move to London, lining up a new job for Emily and schools for the children. Ben informed his mother that he was remaining in Italy to study. He was eighteen and of age, so he was free to choose. That hurt Emily terribly. Erica and Toby didn't want to move to London, but they didn't want to stay with their father. They had all been terribly shaken in the morning by the state of their mother's face and her broken glasses. Riccardo continued in his policy of stubborn denial, threatening to obtain custody of the children. How Emily managed to pack and get to the airport when the time finally came was beyond her.

Emily, believing that the children were under enough stress, had asked Simon not to meet them at the airport when they landed at Heathrow the end of June and had been keeping him at a distance ever since. Mid-August, the kids had started school, and in September, Emily began work at her new job. Tensions between Simon and Emily were high. Simon knew that Riccardo was still harassing Emily over the children despite the distance between them. His phone calls were a source of constant agitation that didn't help the situation. Simon was trying hard to be understanding, but neither one of them was getting any younger. It didn't help matters that Italian law was so excruciatingly slow. It had been a shock for Simon to learn that it would probably take at least three years to finalize Emily's divorce.

The sound of a car horn brought Emily back to the present. Simon had pulled his car over to the curb and was now opening the door for her to climb inside. Today was his birthday. Emily surprised herself by smiling. He was forty-six today. One year younger than she was. A year had passed since the first time they met, and she had never once even bothered to ask his age. Simon caught the brief smile on her face and felt relief. He sensed that this evening was going to be fundamental to their future relationship. Suddenly, all of his plans for the evening shifted.

"You look magnificent."

Emily did look good. She had taken extra pains with her outfit, settling on a simple form-fitting knee-length black cashmere dress and matching cashmere stole, which she had fastened with an elaborate Swarovski broach that glimmered against the black fabric. Beneath the stole, which hung very loosely around her shoulders so that it slid this way and that, exposing all, a slightly lower than usual neckline drew Simon's attention exactly the way that Emily had hoped it would. Her hair was pulled up in a casual bun on top of her head, the work of an understanding young stylist who had been sympathetic to her cause. Tiny tendrils of hair fell teasingly against both sides of her neck. She wore just the faintest hint of makeup, also courtesy of her afternoon session at the beauty salon. She had used every ounce of her knowledge in the art of seduction straight down to the very sexy underwear she was wearing beneath the dress. She knew she was no Italian, but she thought she probably could hold her own against any of the other competition that might be out there.

"You don't look too shabby yourself."

That was an understatement. Simon looked fantastic. He had taken pains with his clothing, too, and was wearing a dark suit with a crisp white shirt, which contrasted nicely with his skin. It was now wasted effort given Simon's new plans for the evening.

"Would you be terribly upset if we cancelled the restaurant and had dinner at my apartment?"

Emily smiled. All of the tension she had been feeling up until that moment instantly vanished. "Hmm. Depends."

"On...?"

"How good of a cook you are and...what you had in mind for dessert."

Simon hit the gas pedal and the car picked up speed. Their relationship was back on track. He pulled his cell phone out of his jacket pocket and began hunting for a number. Emily watched him, amused.

"Sanjay? Simon. If you're manning the phone tonight, who's on tanduri duty?" The man's answer made Simon smile. "Any chance I can convince you to throw together one of your amazing dinners and have it delivered to my place at..." Simon glanced at his watch. It was 6:00 p.m. "Shall we say 8:00? No, for two... Yes, she's very attractive... No, you don't know her yet... I might consider that. No. No dessert." Simon glanced sideways at Emily smiling. "I've already got that covered."

Emily grinned.

It was midnight when Simon very grudgingly accompanied Emily to the door of her apartment. It had been a perfect evening and neither of them wanted it to end, but Emily didn't like the idea of leaving the children alone so late at night. They had reached a compromise that Simon felt he could live with. Emily had consented to tell the children that the two of them were officially dating, which meant that they could see each other on a regular basis.

Emily was scheduled to go to Laos and Cambodia in mid-November. Simon was going to get his mother to take care of the kids, which meant that it was time for Emily to meet her. Emily had also agreed to spend Christmas with Simon. They would have ten days to themselves while the children visited their grandparents and other relatives. They still hadn't decided on a destination but the idea of all that time together gave them something to look forward to.

Meanwhile, although he hadn't said as much to Emily, Simon was going to continue to explore every possible way to speed up the divorce process. Any doubts he might have been having earlier had vanished with the night. Simon walked back into his flat hoping he would still feel Emily's presence in the rooms to counteract the twinge of pain at the idea of sleeping alone. When he finally fell into bed later that morning and caught the faint whiff of Emily's perfume that still lingered there, he pulled the sheets tightly around his body, hugged what he now considered *her* pillow, and slept like a baby, serene in the certainty of the morrow.

From that moment on, life got steadily better. Simon had done an excellent job in choosing schools for Erica and Toby. Despite the fact that Emily had always spoken to her children in English, the truth of the matter was that they had done all of their schooling in Italy and were having some trouble in English. The teachers were all very understanding and the kids felt comfortable with the situation. They had also already made plenty of new friends and were quickly becoming pros at navigating the underground. The novelty of London and life in a major metropolis helped. Erica, in particular, was thrilled.

Once a week and on weekends, Simon was now a regular fixture in their lives. Emily could see that he was going out of his way to win Erica and Toby over, but they were teenagers and, by definition, were not collaborating much. Emily admired Simon's patience. It was a new experience for her to see a man actually take interest in children, and when Simon took Toby to his first soccer game at the end of October and bought tickets to an important dance show for Erica, he was definitely earning points with all of them.

Emily's trip to Laos and Cambodia was scheduled for the last week of November. The second week of November, Simon had to be out of town for work, so they were having dinner at his mother's the third week of November in order for the children to get to know her before Emily took off. They were going to celebrate Thanksgiving American-style.

Emily was extremely nervous about meeting Simon's mother. She worried stupidly about comparisons with Susan, and all of her usual insecurities surfaced. Simon was confident that the two women would get along. For one thing, Simon's mother was American. Like Emily, she had come over to Europe after graduation from college, on a grant for an internship at the BBC, where she met her husband, and had never returned to the States. Babette Russell had worked for the BBC for years, organizing children's programming and other educational programs. Her husband had briefly been a news commentator before moving into management and had then gone into politics. The family spent several years in India, Simon's father acting as cultural attaché at the embassy there. They had returned to England when Simon started secondary school because they felt it was better for their son to study in the UK.

Babette had quit her post at the BBC to follow her husband to India. Upon their return to London, she had thrown herself into London's cultural scene and was actively involved in a number of cultural societies. She also still occasionally consulted with the BBC on special projects. It was clear from the way he talked about her that Simon adored her. Simon's father had passed away shortly after Simon's divorce, and six years later he was still sorely missed.

It was hard not to like Babette Russell. She was like a gusty sea breeze on a summer day. From the minute she opened the door, she had thrown them into a flurry of activities that barely gave Emily time to recover from her initial surprise. She hadn't known that Simon's mother was African-American. Looking at the couple's wedding picture above the fireplace, it was easy to see why. Simon's father had been quintessentially British—ramrod straight hair, ash blond, skin so white and flawless it looked almost albino, and very tall. Simon was virtually a carbon copy of his father. Emily didn't think that Simon was as tall as his father had been, but in every other aspect, there was no doubting his paternity. The only differences that Emily could see were Simon's healthily tanned skin, now fully explained, thick dark hair, and dark eyes. Simon definitely had his mother's beautiful eyes.

Simon entered the living room. Erica and Babette were in one of the upstairs bedrooms trying on evening gowns. Toby was in the back room watching a soccer match. Dinner was over and the evening had been a complete success.

"You look like your father."

"So they say." Simon walked over to where Emily was standing and took her into his arms. The two kissed.

"She likes you, you know."

Emily gave a short laugh. "What makes you say that?"

"Because she is very discreetly giving us time to be alone. If she didn't like you, she would be here obsessively monopolizing the conversation and doing everything in her power to make you uncomfortable."

Emily grinned. "I can't honestly imagine your mother making anyone feel uncomfortable. She's the most affable person I've ever met.
"

"Interesting choice of words. I didn't think people used words like that anymore."

"After twenty years in Italy, I'm sometimes afraid that I'm making them up. Changing Italian words into English ones."

"No. Affable works. So does amiable if you like."

"Amiable." Emily weighed the word carefully. "In Italian that would be *amabile*. Lovable."

"That's what you are." Simon pulled Emily tighter into his arms.

Emily made a face as she wrapped her arms around him. "It doesn't work in that context."

"Hmm." Simon nuzzled her ear. "There are plenty of other adjectives I can think of to describe the way I feel about you." His mouth traced its way to the base of her neck but, just as he was making his way back toward her mouth, they heard movements upstairs that told them their quiet time together was going to be short-lived. Simon sighed and hugged Emily briefly. As he let her go, his eyes fell on a picture of his parents. He reached over and picked it up.

"This is my favorite." The picture was of Simon's mom and dad at a restaurant. It was obvious that they didn't know they were being photographed at the time it was taken. They were both staring into each other's eyes. The photographer had captured a private moment between two people obviously in love. The emotion emanated out to the viewer. The picture was poignantly beautiful.

"It was their twenty-fifth wedding anniversary. They were on a cruise. One of the other passengers on the ship saw them at dinner and couldn't resist taking their picture. She had it developed the next day and gave it to them as a present."

Emily was silent as she examined the couple. Her heart skipped a beat, and she placed her hand absentmindedly on the glass. "That's the way it's supposed to be," she sighed.

Before Simon could answer, his mother and Erica were entering the room. Emily moved self-consciously away. Simon put the picture back on the mantle. Erica practically waltzed into the room. Emily smiled. It had been awhile since she had seen such exuberant happiness on her daughter's face.

"Mom! You have to see the dresses Mrs. Russell wants to give to me. They're beautiful!"

"I told her she could have them if it was all right with you. They belonged to my one of my nieces but she's outgrown them all. My sister-in-law didn't have the heart to throw them out, and I had room in the upstairs closet so they've been there for awhile now. She was a championess in competitive ballroom dancing. Some of her costumes were really tacky, to be perfectly honest. I only kept the more elegant ones."

As she was speaking, Erica dashed over to where her mother was standing and began pulling her excitedly toward the stairs.

"Come and see."

"Erica. Don't be rude. It's getting late," Emily chided.

"I don't think Toby's game has finished yet," Simon interceded.

"It's really not a problem for me. If Erica takes them off of my hands, I'll finally be able to make use of the space."

"Okay," Emily capitulated. "Let's go take a look."

The rest of the evening passed in a blur. When they left the house, Erica had three large shopping bags full of dresses that she and Simon lugged out to the car. Toby was happy because his favorite team had won the match and it had been a really good game. Emily was more than happy and couldn't help smiling to herself all the way home.

If there was one cloud in their relationship during that period, it was Emily's struggle with religion. Emily still considered herself Catholic and since she was still technically married she felt she was committing adultery. Emily had found an Italian Catholic church shortly after her arrival in London, St. Peter's, that she went to with the children on a regular basis. It had taken her a few weeks to get up the courage to talk with one of the priests but she now had regular conversations about life and confession. Father Dominic was fairly liberal so, although he couldn't officially condone Emily's divorce, he didn't condemn her either. However, much to Simon's chagrin, he did try to convince Emily that her best path at the moment was abstinence. She couldn't confess to adultery if she continued to see Simon biblically. Emily agreed that confession was profoundly serious and could only be followed by an act of true repentance. To give up Simon was something she wasn't prepared to do so she did her best to keep their physical relationship to a minimum and, more importantly, keep it away from the children. So, although Simon would have spent the night at Emily's, on more than one occasion he was reluctantly forced to admit defeat and head for home.

That night after dinner with his mother was one of those occasions. Simon hit the light switch and looked around his empty flat, feeling somewhat frustrated. He pulled his phone out of his pocket and hit speed dial as he lowered himself down onto the couch. Jeff's familiar voice came on at the other end. He was singing, "I can't get no satisfaction" by the Rolling Stones. Simon didn't know whether to grind his teeth or laugh.

"Why on earth do I put up with you?"

"You call me at 11:30 p.m. and you actually have the gall to ask me why you put up with me! It's a good thing my puppy here is fast asleep."

"How's your kitten?"

"Purring away. You realize, of course, that Fatima hinted that I ought to get an unlisted number."

"You wouldn't go along with that, would you?"

"What? And miss out on all of your charming pathos? Not a chance! You know, I'm going to have to actually thank Emily when I see her. You've called me more in these past few months than you have in years. It's quite enjoyable. Or would be if you weren't always so depressed."

"I'm not depressed."

"No. Tonight you've just got a hard-on!"

"I'm hanging up!"

"Don't you dare! If you're going to call me at this time of night, you'd better bloody well be prepared to let me have a little fun. So what's tonight's topic?"

For the next quarter of an hour Simon dove into his feelings, expressing his frustration at Emily's being Catholic and not being able to get anywhere with her divorce proceedings. Jeff asked whether or not she could get an annulment, but Simon had already looked into that, and he didn't seem to be able to make any headway with the Vatican bureaucracy.

As they were winding up their conversation, Jeff told Simon, "Cheer up. At least Emily hasn't asked you to convert yet."

"If I thought it would help, I'd convert tomorrow."

"Ah. I'd have to start calling you Napoleon after that," Jeff chirped. "Paris, or Emily in this case, vaut bien un messe."

Simon shook his head. "You've got your facts wrong. That was Henry the IV of Bourbon."

"They're all too French for me. I'd still rather call you Napoleon. It sounds better. Although some bourbon might help you sleep."

Simon chuckled. "Take care of yourself."

"Ditto my friend."

Emily left for Laos on Sunday afternoon. Simon had a business meeting in Paris on Monday and Tuesday, but on Wednesday he told his mom he would be joining her for supper. When he got to their apartment, he found everyone at the dining room table doing homework.

"Just in time," his mother told him. "Toby's got a math equation that we can't figure out."

So, while Simon worked with Toby on his math, his mother went over Erica's English essay with her. It was an entirely new experience for Simon and one he found he enjoyed enormously. Supper was a lively affair. Babette had taken the kids to see *Fame* on a last-minute deal the night before, and they were still drunk with excitement, filling Simon in on every minute detail. After supper, Babette suggested they all play Scrabble.

Five minutes into the game, Simon was able to appreciate just how intelligent the children were but he was also able to gauge the gap in their language skills. He could have won hands down, but he found himself suggesting words and surreptitiously cheating to give the children a fighting chance against his mother. Babette won, but the kids had a great time and demanded a rematch for the following day so Thursday evening was more of the same, and Simon promised himself that it would become a regular event.

Friday, Erica came home with an invitation to a party. Emily was already traveling so there was no way to ask her permission. Simon and his mother had to make the decision. They decided that Emily could go as long as she let Simon accompany her and pick her up at 11:30 p.m. Erica had been hoping to stay out until midnight but since the alternative was staying at home, she accepted with relatively good grace. Toby and Babette were going to the cinema, so after Simon dropped Erica off at her party, he headed to the gym for a workout.

As Simon was pulling up to the curb, he caught sight of Erica in what looked like a rather passionate embrace on the front steps. Since the road wasn't heavily trafficked, he waited discreetly for a pause before tapping lightly on the car horn. Erica nearly jumped out of her skin, quickly said her goodbyes, ran to the car, and slid in beside Simon, her eyes downcast. Simon thought she was blushing - just like her mother. It was hard to tell in the dark.

After a few minutes of silence, Erica asked softly, "You're not going to tell my mom, are you?"

Simon thought carefully before he replied. "That's an interesting question. It implies that you think you may have been doing something wrong or something that you know your mother wouldn't approve of. That was always my rule of thumb when I was your age. I always asked myself 'would I be embarrassed if my parents found out about this?' If the answer was yes, I wouldn't do it. I didn't want to lose their respect."

Erica was silent the rest of the way home. As Simon accompanied her to the door, he said, "Erica. There's nothing wrong with two people being in love or expressing their love if that's the way they feel about each other, but sometimes, particularly when you're young, it's hard to distinguish passion from true love. It's just something to think about."

Erica nodded and let herself into the flat where Babette was waiting for her.

Emily came in the next day, utterly exhausted and totally content. The trip had gone even better than she could have imagined. Simon had pulled a few strings to get Emily hired at the agency she was now working for. It was a small company that specialized in higher education for women in third-world countries. Emily had been asked to put together a curriculum on marketing and had actually gone to Laos and Cambodia to hold her first seminars on the topic. She had spent the week in two tiny jungle towns illustrating marketing techniques and website development to two cooperatives of women. She had received nothing but praise for her work, and she was floating on clouds as she glided off the plane. Simon was waiting for her when she came out of Customs and whisked her off to his flat. The children were with his mother for the afternoon, and they would all meet up for supper.

The days were much shorter now. The weather had turned exceptionally cold. Christmas was almost upon them. Simon and Emily still hadn't decided where they were going to spend their time in Italy. Emily was extremely nervous about leaving the children with their grandparents, but she knew there was nothing she could do about it.

That irrational fear was probably what was blocking her from making a decision.

Jeff called toward mid-December and basically took matters into his own hands. He had been offered a new assignment with the embassy in Rome and Fatima had actually agreed to the change. He and Fatima were going to spend Christmas and New Year's in Rome so that they could get a feel for the city and make arrangements for their move.

Simon's only comment had been, "You do realize, of course, that this means I'll be spending a lot of time at masses."

Jeffrey had chuckled. "When in Rome... Just remember, you're doing it for the sex. Whatever it takes to keep the ladies happy, Simon, my good man. Because when they're happy, I guarantee that you'll be happy, too."

Christmas in Rome was magic. Despite Simon's predictions, Emily's religious obligations were more than satisfied with midnight mass. Simon had to admit that it was a very good show. The days with Jeff and Fatima flew by. Jeff was constantly exuberant. Fatima was playfully impertinent, and Emily couldn't remember when she had laughed harder or enjoyed herself as much. Simon was in seventh heaven.

On the twenty-ninth of December, Emily and Fatima met the two men at the bar in the lobby. The two women were just returning from a shopping expedition. Simon and Jeff were in earnest conversation. Emily heard Jeff say, "It couldn't hurt."

"What couldn't hurt?" Fatima wanted to know.

"To give you ladies our credit cards and let you back out for more shopping. That's the second time this trip you've come back empty-handed, pet. Could it be all those years of training have finally paid off?" Jeff gave his wife a friendly squeeze.

"You're not planning on working, are you, Mr. Kinkade? I thought we had an agreement."

"Fatima." Jeff began with his usual theatrics. "Love of my life. My angel. My pet. Would I do a thing like that? 'Tis the season to be jolly. Simon and I have been on our very best behavior this whole trip. Any work I've done has been for our future here, and Simon's been very sweet playing Romeo to Emily's Juliette. Simon and I just thought we'd take the afternoon off and run some errands of our own, if you don't mind."

During his speech, Emily had sidled over to Simon, who put his arms around her and kissed the top of her head. She was now looking at him expectantly.

"Do you mind?" Simon asked fondly.

"And wherefore goest thou, pray tell?" Emily asked archly.

"Top secret," Jeff butted in. "A man has a right to his privacy. Unless he's happily married, which means," and he swooped over to give his wife a quick peck on the cheek, "I'll tell you tonight. And you," he turned to Emily grinning wickedly, "You, wanton hussy, will just have to use your feminine wiles to find out." He winked at Simon. "Won't that be fun. Something to look forward to tonight. Right, that's settled then. You girls go on and have lunch together and then go back out and buy to your heart's content. Simon and I will be back before seven and will wine you and dine you with whatever is left of our money."

Emily laughingly reminded him, "I do work, you know."

"Good girl. Then Simon won't mind picking up the tab on dinner tonight. Ta-ta and toodles." And with that, he practically drove his friend out of the building. The two women watched them leave, amused and very curious to know what they were up to. They talked it over briefly, agreeing that it probably had something to do with New Year's Eve. Emily's children, including Ben, would be joining them on the thirty-first, and they had all talked about that evening's entertainment repeatedly without ever coming to a firm decision. It would be typical of Jeff to organize something mildly elaborate and for Simon to go along with the scheme.

Emily and Fatima didn't really feel like going back out so they spent the afternoon in the hotel being lazy. Emily went to the gym where she did a light workout and had a sauna. Back in the room, she took a leisurely shower, then, wrapped in nothing but a hotel bathrobe, she curled up on the bed to read a book and fell fast asleep. Simon enjoyed waking her up.

The rest of their stay in Rome passed so quickly that Emily never had time to ask Simon about how he spent his afternoon with Jeff.

Emily got very emotional with Ben. He had to promise to come and visit her in London for Easter break. Emily was so wrapped up in her own emotions that she didn't notice the slight change in Simon's; otherwise, she might have caught the subtle glint in his eyes and recognized the faint hint of optimistic determination that he was doing his best to conceal.

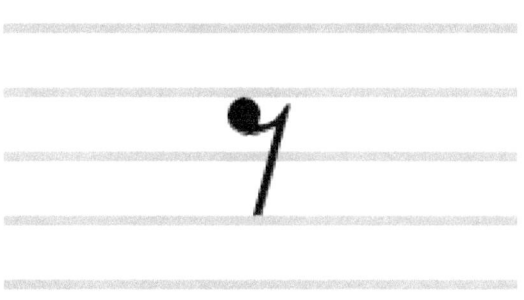

The New Year got off to a roaring start, and it was March before they even knew it. Back in London, Emily was still being fastidiously Catholic, but Simon was now doing his best to accommodate her. He even accompanied Emily to mass most Sundays. To his surprise, he actually found the sense of community enjoyable. Jeff and Fatima moved to Rome at the beginning of February and, if possible, the two men spoke even more often than before—so often that even Emily noticed.

Simon kept his promise, and Scrabble was now a regular evening event when he was in town. Babette also became a permanent fixture in their lives. Dinners at her house were frequent. The children often spent the afternoons with her, initially to get help with their homework, but they enjoyed her company so much that they always stayed on to chat.

The more Simon got to know the children, the more he regretted that he and Emily hadn't met earlier. He was very glad that he had never had children with Susan but he thought that a child with Emily might have been different. He was grateful for the opportunity Emily's children provided. It was a new experience and he genuinely liked it.

Emily's birthday in March coincided with Easter and, as promised, Ben flew in for the occasion. Ben was extremely easygoing and fit into their lives as if he had always been there. His brother and sister were ecstatic as they proudly took him to all of their favorite places, navigating the underground like true Londoners.

Emily was so happy, Simon thought she would quite literally burst. She was forty-nine. Simon felt the usual pang of frustration. Who knew how much time they had left to spend together? He sincerely hoped and prayed that the new course of action he and Jeff had started in Rome would pay off.

In April, Simon flew to Rome. Officially, he was working. Unofficially, he had a series of very important appointments at the Vatican. When Simon came back from Rome, he was formally Catholic. He didn't say anything to Emily. It had been a very surreal experience. He had been baptized, had first communion, and had been confirmed all in the same day. He had then spoken to so many cardinals and clerics that he lost count. He and Jeff both made conspicuous donations to the church and presented the formal paperwork on financing for a water project that would also benefit an important mission in Africa. Simon had protested when Jeff made his own personal contribution at the end of Simon's confirmation ceremony, but Jeffrey merely laughed and told him he was getting all of his anniversary presents in advance just in case he ever became senile. Simon tried to reason with him because the church hadn't given them any guarantees, but Jeff was convinced that Emily would soon be divorced.

The road from here to there was fairly convoluted. Emily needed an annulment and Simon needed to be Catholic. The church, thanks to the very large sums of money that had been donated on its behalf, now felt that Simon and Emily were worthy of divine intervention. Simon never knew precisely how they did it, but at 10:35 a.m. on the eighteenth of June he received an express package from Rome. It was the paperwork confirming Emily's annulment plus official transcripts of Simon's baptism, communion, and confirmation.

The emotions that overcame him in that precise moment as he sat there staring at the papers in front of him were something Simon would never forget. When he felt he had sufficient control of himself, he took a deep breath and dialed Jeff.

"Well, hullo, Napoleon!" Jeff sniggered.

"Jeff…" But Simon was at a loss for words and didn't know what else to say.

"What are you doing on the phone snivelling like a sissy? You have to get out there and win your lady love. She's a free bird now; she might just fly the coop. You never know. And I'm not going through this again. It cost me a pretty penny. I think I lost three hairs in the ordeal, too, and I owe half the Italian cleric a favor. So get off the phone and go win the fair maiden's hand. Oh, and you can tell Emily from me that the two of you are now fully eligible for a steady flow of guilt-free sex, so I don't want anymore late-night calls unless you want to talk dirty to me." And he hung up.

The day couldn't pass quickly enough for Simon. It was virtually impossible for him to concentrate. He kept going over scenario after scenario trying to determine his best plan of attack. He really did feel like Napoleon facing his Waterloo. Emily was speaking at a late afternoon tea that the St. Peter's parish had organized. She was going to talk about her recent experiences teaching women in developing countries. Simon had agreed to pick up Erica and Toby and meet her there. Simon decided to tackle the children first. He knew they were fundamental to his success.

Toby opened the door. "Hi, Simon. You're early. Erica is still doing her hair."

Simon gripped the envelope of papers he was holding, suddenly nervous. "That's all right. How was your day?"

Toby shrugged his shoulders and led the way back into the living room where he had been playing with the Wii. He automatically began saving his game and putting everything away. Simon watched in silence.

Toby had just flopped back down onto the couch when Erica walked into the room.

"You look really nice."

Toby moved to get up but Simon stopped him. "Wait a second, Toby. There's…something I want to talk to the two of you about. Erica. Would you sit for a minute?"

Simon looked at the two children. Erica had just turned sixteen. Toby was twelve. They weren't babies. Simon decided on a direct approach.

"These," he held up the envelope, "are your mother's divorce papers. Your mother and father are…officially divorced. I think you probably know how I feel about your mother, but just in case you have any doubts on the subject, I want you both to know that I love her very much. Actually, I care about all of you very much, and I want us to be together…like a family."

Neither Toby nor Erica spoke. They stared at him in stony silence. Simon recognized their discomfort, but he took courage in the fact that they weren't running to their rooms in protest.

Simon took another breath; now came the hard part. "There's…one more thing I need to say…to tell you. I'm…" He struggled to find the right words. "…desperately tired of hiding my feelings in front of you, and I want to be with you and your mother every single moment I'm allowed." Simon paused and then told them the most important part. "That includes sleeping here."

Erica threw herself off the couch as if it were on fire. "Ew. Gross!"

Toby's entire face formed an astonished O. "You mean you want to have *sex* with our mother?"

Erica raced toward the front door. "Toby! Can we please go now? We're going to be late!"

Simon had to make a concentrated effort to hide his amusement, particularly at Toby's blunt reaction. He rose gingerly from the couch. "Right. I'll leave these in the kitchen and we'll be off." Erica stormed out the door in protest. Toby waited for Simon out on the landing so that he could lock the door. They didn't say anything until they were almost at the church and then Simon told them, "Your mother doesn't know yet."

"She doesn't know you want to have *sex* with her?"

"Toby! Che cavolo dici." And Erica broke into a tirade of Italian that didn't stop until the car was parked. Erica jumped out of the car and stormed toward the parish hall.

Simon pulled Toby short before he took off after his sister. "Toby, for the record, what your mother and I do behind closed doors is our business. Just don't be too surprised when I start showing up for breakfast."

Toby raised his shoulders and threw his hands up into the air, looking suddenly very Italian. "Hey, it's not my business."

Simon ruffled his hair. "Good man. Thanks."

Emily's talk went very well. There were about twenty people in the room, and everyone stayed for the sandwiches and tea at the end. Emily noticed that the kids were out of sorts, but she put it down to the fact that they had been forced to come and listen to her speak. Simon was quiet, too. He was preparing for the final battle in his own personal Waterloo.

As soon as they got back to the flat, Erica raced to her room, shutting the doors noisily behind her. Toby threw himself down on the couch and turned on the television. Simon followed Emily into the kitchen where she pulled a kettle out for some herbal tea, but before she could put it on the stove, Simon picked up the envelope he had left on the table and silently handed it to her.

Emily put the kettle down, looking at him questioningly. "What's this?"

"Why don't you open it and see?"

Emily took the envelope from him and glanced at the documents. It took her a couple of minutes to realize what she was looking at. Her gaze flew repeatedly from the papers in her hands to Simon's face. She was stunned. She tried to speak.

"How?"

Simon shook his head softly *no* and moved to take her face between his hands. "It's a long story. Emily, it's official. You are a free woman. Marry me."

Emily's mind couldn't quite take it all in. Simon kissed her. Instinctively, Emily yielded into his arms but after a few moments she remembered the children in the other room and tried to pull away. Simon relinquished his hold on her lips, but he had no intention of surrendering his position.

"Simon. The children are…"

"They already know."

"Know?"

Simon pulled Emily softly closer, lifting her face gently to his, his hand cupping her chin as he spoke. "They know that I love you. That I want to marry you and…" Simon drew a breath. "…that I have no intention of going home tonight or any other night for the rest of my life."

Emily gasped, her eyes widening in shock. Simon could see the storm of emotions brewing behind her face, a mixture of awe and annoyance at his audacity. He knew he had to be quick if he wanted to ensure his victory tonight. Simon began an all-out assault. "Emily, from the first moment that I held you in my arms, I knew I wanted to be with you for the rest of my life. Every second that I spend with you, I'm happy. Happier than I've ever been in my whole entire life. You are everything that I need. That I desire. I honestly don't think that I could live without you. If you feel the same way about me, you won't send me home tonight. I can't go back to my flat now that I know you're free. Emily, this isn't adultery anymore. This is a man and a woman expressing their feelings for each other."

Simon took her face gently in both hands. "In my heart, I couldn't be more married to you than I am tonight. You are the only reason I get up in the morning. Emily, all I'm asking is that your face be the last thing I see every night before I drift to sleep and the first thing I see every morning. Please." His hands slid down her body, his lips softly brushing hers, and then suddenly he was kissing her everywhere.

Later, Emily would only vaguely remember the short trip down the hallway to her bedroom. Emily got up briefly at eleven to send Toby to bed. She was extremely embarrassed but, strangely, knowing that Simon was in the other room waiting for her, and would be for the rest of her life, made it reasonably tolerable. She was sure they would all get used to it eventually. Simon woke up at the crack of dawn and, satisfied that he had faced his Waterloo and been victorious, graciously decided to leave before the children woke up, promising to be back for breakfast or shortly thereafter since it was Saturday and they had the whole day to spend together.

Simon slipped into the flat and their lives effortlessly. When he was in town, which was becoming more and more frequent as he passed on assignments that took him away from London for long periods of time, evenings were spent in just about the same way they always had been, only more so. There were evenings with Babette, Scrabble tournaments, homework, and movies. Breakfast had been awkward at first. Simon quickly learned to put pygama bottoms on when he got caught early one morning on his way to the kitchen in his underwear. The only major novelty for the children was watching their mother be happy. The wedding was scheduled for September. Father Dominic had insisted that Emily and Simon take a marriage preparation course, so the two had settled on a date at the end of September, the anniversary of their first night together.

Mid-September, Simon got a phone call from Susan asking him to meet her for a drink after work. It had been months since the last time they had spoken. Simon had basically forgotten about her, wrapped up as he was in his new life. The pub was dark and crowded when Simon walked in. Susan was already there at a table in the corner. He noticed that she looked tired.

"Hey."

"Hey, yourself. You look tired."

Susan shrugged self-consciously. "It's been a rough couple of weeks."

"Sorry to hear that." Simon sat down.

"You look great, on the other hand. It's been awhile. What have you been up to?"

Simon smiled, realizing that he had never spoken to Susan about his relationship with Emily. His smiled widened as he remembered their conversations together on the subject back in Istanbul. He was actually looking forward to being made fun of when Susan blurted out, "Richard and I broke up."

Simon was instantly somber. He wasn't quite sure what he was supposed to say, but before he could formulate a reply, the waitress appeared with two drinks. Simon raised his eyes slightly but didn't say anything. It was typical of Susan to order for him. Beer. Not his favorite but it would do. Simon eyed Susan warily, waiting for her to speak. He took a couple of swigs while Susan toyed with hers, her eyes darting around the pub nervously.

She gave a sharp laugh. "Actually, he left me. Apparently he fell head over heels in lust for one of our new interns. Now she's pregnant and they're getting married."

Simon sucked in his breath. "I'm really sorry, Suz."

Susan took a swallow of beer and then spit out. "She's not even thirty!"

Simon shook his head and looked slowly around the pub at a loss for words, trying his best to reign in his happiness to match her mood. It wasn't easy. His mind wandered. He found himself comparing the two women and was surprised to discover that he felt little more than compassion for Susan. He tried to remember what he had ever seen in Susan, but he couldn't. Emily and the children were his life now. Simon had always been a one-woman man. He turned back to face the woman in front of him.

"I'm not sure I'm the right shoulder to cry on, Suz, except for the fact that I never really cared for the man. As I recall, he's one of the reasons you left me."

Susan was quiet for a moment, looking down into her half-empty glass. "I was wondering whether or not he couldn't be the reason you and I got back together." She said it so quietly Simon almost thought he hadn't heard her correctly, but when she raised her gaze to meet his it was like being struck by lightning.

He said the first thing that came to mind, "I'm getting married at the end of the month."

Now it was Susan's turn to be shocked. She stared at him wordlessly, surprise and chagrin written into every line of expression. A veteran improviser, she searched desperately for something to say. Simon threw down the rest of his beer and stood up.

"I should probably be going."

Susan blocked him before he could get out the door. "Simon, wait! I'm sorry. I didn't mean to be so selfish. You're getting married. That's wonderful news. I'm so happy for you. Really, I mean that. I'm just a little…confused…right now. Please. Forget what I just said. Who is she? Where did you meet? When's the big day?" Susan forced a smile.

Simon hesitated for a fraction of a second and then decided that it was pointless to hide anything from Susan. "Actually, you already know her. I'm marrying Emily White on the twenty-third."

Susan's jaw dropped to her waist. "Emily…*White*?"

Simon smiled in spite of himself then he bent down to give Susan a quick kiss on the cheek. "Be happy, Suz," he said, and left.

Emily was waiting for him when he got home.

"So, how was your drink with Susan?"

"Hmm… She didn't know I was getting married."

"How did she take the news?"

Simon decided it would be okay to lie since he was basically telling the truth. He pulled Emily into his arms, his face softening as he gazed sincerely into her eyes. "She ranted and raved and begged me to take her back but when I told her I was marrying the most beautiful, intelligent, most extraordinary woman in the world, she wished us both well." Simon kissed Emily, nuzzling her neck, then continued, "I also told her that we couldn't be friends any more because Jeffrey was too jealous."

Emily snuggled closer. "Blame it on Jeffrey if you will, but I won't complain either."

"I assumed as much. I usually follow my gut instinct when I'm closing a deal."

"Am I a deal, then?"

"The best deal of my life."

The wedding was a very simple affair. Just intimate family and friends. Simon had insisted that Emily wear a traditional gown and veil for the occasion, and she had found a very simple wedding dress in organza and chiffon with hand-sewn beadwork in soft antique white and cream that showed her figure off to perfection. She looked heavenly.

Simon was dashing in his evening wear, very appropriate for their four o'clock wedding. Babette had taken care of all the other details. They had an elegant buffet dinner catered to her home with live music. How she got the waiters, the quartet, and all of the guests to fit into her living room was beyond Simon. He barely noticed anyway. He couldn't take his eyes off Emily. At one point in the evening, Jeff handed him a pair of dark sunglasses, telling him to put them on because the beams of light streaming out of his eyes every time he looked at his new wife were starting to give him a headache. It was useless, of course, because Emily gleamed even more than Simon and nothing could shade her glow.

Vivace

Emily and Simon both had busy schedules in October and November so they decided to postpone their honeymoon until December, and they decided it was going to be a family affair. Simon wanted everyone to participate in his happiness. Certain that Emily felt the same way too, he called Jeffrey to organize a Caribbean cruise at Christmas for the entire tribe.

Riccardo, embroiled in a complicated new relationship, was surprisingly willing to let the children go with their mother. That was how Simon, Emily, Toby, Erica, Ben, Jeffrey, and Fatima, together with their son Umar, and Babette all found themselves sitting on the sundeck sipping various drinks Christmas day.

The cruise was a wonderful experience for all of them, but one of the most memorable nights was the Bob Marley reggae party. When the lounge singer started crooning "No Woman, No Cry," Jeffrey jumped to his feet, pulling Simon with him and began singing along, first swaying to the beat then pseudo-dancing. The children would have been embarrassed if it hadn't been so funny. Tired of dancing with Simon, Jeffrey tried to convince Fatima to join him, but she stubbornly refused. Simon had little trouble convincing Emily to dance with him; after all, she was on her honeymoon.

From that night on, for the rest of the cruise, they were regulars in the lounge. On Spanish night, Jeffrey dragged Simon to the floor for an impromptu tango. When the music turned to flamenco, Emily surprised them all with a very convincing impersonation of a Spanish dancer, earning the applause of everyone around them.

On New Year's Eve, the company split up. The children all went to the disco. Babette retired early, claiming she was tired. Emily, Simon, Jeffrey, and Fatima celebrated in the lounge. Shortly after midnight, the two women decided they had had enough. Simon and Jeffrey asked to stay in the lounge a little longer. Jeffrey probably had had one drink too many and decided it was time to indoctrinate his friend in the secrets to a successful marriage.

"Ah, Simon, my friend! You realize of course that sooner or later the honeymoon is going to be over, and I don't mean just on this ship. One morning you're going to wake up and discover that your fair lady farts, pardon my French, just like the rest of us. You're going to have to learn to love her for her faults no matter how stinky they are."

"Jeffrey, I think you're drunk."

"No. See, that's another problem. That's a fact, and women don't want plain facts."

"I didn't know you were a woman."

"You're confusing me."

"Maybe I'm just intentionally misunderstanding."

"Oh-oh, you're good."

"Thank you."

"There you go. *Thank you* is good. So are *please* and *I'm sorry. I love you* never hurts either."

"I love you."

"I know you do, but you have to say it to her. Tell your wife you love her at least once a day. Twice on Sundays."

"Only twice on Sundays?"

"It's a religious holiday. Have some respect."

"Right."

"Don't forget you're Catholic now."

"I'm not complaining."

"That's good, too. Never complain. Complaining is bad. And remember, even when she's wrong, she's right."

"I think I've heard that one before."

"Yeah, well, what about dancing with her every now and then?"

"Dancing?

"Absolutely. Only not while she's cooking. It drives them nuts."

Simon threw back his head and laughed at that one.

"Any other words of advice, O master-of-the-art?"

"Don't be impertinent. Need I remind you that your first marriage ended in divorce?"

"Ouch. No need to get nasty."

"The carrot and stick. That works with men. It doesn't work as well with women. They're only happy with carrots…or maybe its carats, as in diamonds. I forget."

"You ought to try giving Fatima a carrot on a string and see whether she'll wear it or tries to stick it up your bum."

Jeffrey sniggered. "I love it when you talk dirty to me. One last word of advice. This is the most important piece of advice I can give you. Learn to love shopping."

"Okay. That's it. I'm sending you to bed."

"She's a good woman, your Emily."

"I know she is."

"Not many women would go on their honeymoon with their husband's best friend."

"They would if that best friend were you."

"Isn't that sweet. Now you're trying to butter me up. The drinks have already been paid for and I'll not pay a farthing more."

"Say goodnight, Jeff."

"Goodnight Jeff."

"Think you can make it to your cabin, or do I have to carry you?"

Jeff sniggered again. "I'd like to see you try." And with that, he blew Simon a kiss and staggered away. Simon watched him for a minute, gauging whether or not Jeffrey needed his help, but Jeffrey wasn't that drunk. Simon smiled and headed toward his suite where he snuggled next to Emily under the covers. She was already fast asleep.

Simon didn't need Jeffrey's advice. He already meant to do everything in his power to make this marriage last. He was certain he wouldn't get another chance. Simon was going to be forty-eight in the new year, and his priorities in life had been realigned. Being away from home for work, for example, was now a burden. He missed Emily. He missed the children.

Emily only had four missions per year, one per quarter. Those were slightly more acceptable because he got to stay home with Erica and Toby. Simon never asked the children to call him dad, and he never pretended to be their father. He was simply there for them, filling the role. The fact that the children avoided calling him by his first name was a subtle tribute to how well he was doing in the part.

In May, Simon was offered a tenured teaching position at a London university in economics. It meant less travelling, more time with his new family. It was a major career change that Simon gladly embraced. There were other changes that year, too.

The lease was up on the flat. Babette suggested that she move into Simon's place, which was currently vacant, leaving her Georgian-style house to her son. The house had always been too big for her and, now that she was getting older, she thought it was time to make a move while she was still young enough to adapt. It had been an exhausting ordeal, but they were already settled in when the first rays of summer peeped through the living room windows.

There was a hint of melancholy in the thought that Erica wouldn't be staying in her new room long. Emily had fretted that Erica would want to return to Italy after secondary school, but she had been selected at Cambridge and had decided it was too good an opportunity to pass up. Emily contented herself with the knowledge that her daughter could always come home on the weekends.

Teaching suited Simon. He loved the one-on-one time with his students. He was still consulting, but his class schedule kept him close to home most of the year. He started a steady correspondence with Emily's son Ben. Ben was studying economics in Italy, and Simon often asked his opinion on materials and topics he thought might be of interest. Time passed.

Emily's fiftieth birthday party was a huge event. The usual crowd was there, including Jeffrey and Fatima, who flew in for the occasion. Simon had also invited several of Emily's colleagues and other acquaintances. Jeffrey had organized a very elaborate set of presents to help Emily enter her golden years in style—everything from denture gel to a plaster cast of boobs.

"What on earth are these for?" Emily laughed.

"Well, you know. If that husband of yours ever complains that your upper body parts aren't quite as firm and fresh as he remembers them, you can always pull this out and show him that your boobs are as firm as ever!"

"Jeffrey! You're impossible."

Simon hugged her playfully. "Don't worry. You'll never need it."

Emily shook her head wryly. "You never know."

The last package in the box was Viagra. Emily had tears streaming down her face, she was laughing so hard.

"I thought this was for men."

"It is. That's so that hubby dear always performs according to specification. You can put it in his soup if you like, although they say it works better on an empty stomach."

Simon grabbed the vial out of Emily's hand and tossed it at his friend.

"Take it back; we won't be needing it."

"That's not for you to decide. This is Emily's present, not yours. I'd count them if I were you. There's nothing there that says she has to use them with you."

Simon virtually growled and then pulled his wife into a very passionate kiss that had the whole room cheering. When they pulled apart, they were both a little breathless. As they stood there staring into each other's eyes, Jeffrey brought the attention back to the presents.

"Well, it's a good thing I thought to buy the dental gel. If you're going to suck her teeth out like that she's going to need it before the night is through. Go on and open the other presents, Emily. Let's see if there's anything else that might be useful."

Emily opened Simon's present last. It was a very simple stylized gold cross on a gold chain.

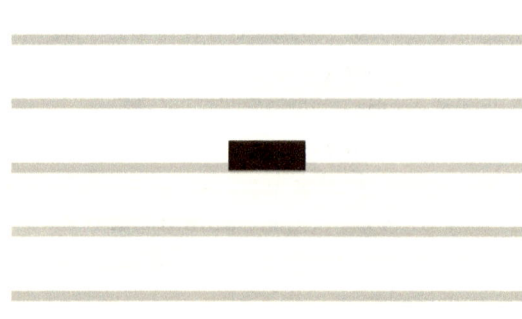

Mid-April, Emily had to go to Nigeria for one of her courses. Both she and Simon were nervous about the trip. The village she was going to was in a relatively quiet part of the country, but tensions were always high and unrest was unpredictable. The course was being sponsored by the United Nations, and the organizers felt that, with the right precautions, there shouldn't be any problems in getting Emily to and from the village. Through the church, Emily discovered that there was a mission nearby and exchanged emails with the priest there, who assured her that the area was quiet. It was only four days; what could possibly happen?

The day before Emily was to return home, the village was brutally attacked by rebels. Emily had been invited to the mission to spend the morning with the children to teach them songs in English. If they had been in the outdoor classroom, Emily probably would have been killed instantly, along with the children. The nuns, out of courtesy to Emily, had organized her session with the children in the mission's recreation room, which also served as the cafeteria. It was the only room that had air conditioning.

The rebels burst into the village firing their rifles randomly this way and that, sending everyone outside into a frenzy of pandemonium. The carnage was incredible. Men and boys were shot. Women were raped and beaten. Macherie's mother was one of these.

Six men pounced on her as she tried frantically to make her way toward the cafeteria. Emily witnessed the scene, horrified, from the window but was saved from seeing more than her being hauled across a table by a bullet that shattered the glass in the window where Emily was standing. Emily's glasses protected her eyes, but she was cut in the face.

Emily, several of the nuns, and a young priest began frantically trying to protect the children. The priests and two older nuns began dragging heavy furniture over to block the door. Emily and the other nun began overturning tables to make a makeshift fort to hide behind. Macherie was the youngest child in the room. Emily scooped her up, but before she could get her behind the tables, another volley of fire was shot into the room. Emily threw herself backward into a corner, squeezing between the wall and a metal cabinet, trying to ball herself around little Macherie as much as possible. One of the older nuns fell on top of the children. She had been shot through the head.

Emily had no idea how long the carnage went on, or why the rebels never bothered to enter the building. Macherie clung to her in silence, but Emily could hear the other children whimpering and crying, some of them possibly wounded. Even after the silence returned to the village, Emily remained where she was. They all did. They listened for what seemed like hours, terrified that the rebels might return.

They heard someone scratching at the door. Soft moaning noises were coming from other directions. Cautiously, everyone came back to life. The young priest who had hidden under one of the desks blocking the door was miraculously still alive. He began removing the furniture from in front of the door. No one had the courage to go toward the window and look out. Emily could do very little to help anyone. Macherie wouldn't let go of her grip. Emily spoke to the children, trying to tell them that everything was going to be all right. She prayed to God that it was true.

The sight that met them when they opened the door was something Emily would never forget. Macherie's mother, her mangled body bleeding profusely from several places, had dragged her way to the door and was now trying desperately to raise herself to come inside, her face frantically searching for Macherie's. Macherie began screaming and crying for her mother; she was so wild that Emily had no choice but to put her down. The priest did his best to lift the woman and drag her further into the room. Macherie threw herself on top of the woman. Emily knelt beside her. The woman said something to Macherie and pushed her toward Emily. Macherie went limp, and Emily instinctively scooped her up, holding her tight. The two women stared at each other in silence for a moment, then Macherie's mother reached for Emily's hand and pulled it toward her.

"Take her," she said. "Take Ma…cherie." And she was gone.

Emily started to rattle and shake. If it hadn't been for little Macherie trembling in her arms, she would have fallen to pieces. Emily looked blindly around her, her eyes and ears gradually focusing on the nightmare outside. She could hear women crying somewhere. She staggered to her feet, Macherie still in her arms. Emily turned her attention to the other children. It was a miracle. Of the sixteen people in the room, only the nun had been killed. Two of the children were wounded. The rest were unscratched. The village, on the other hand, had been decimated. For most of the afternoon, the survivors wandered aimlessly in search of family and friends. Emily sat quietly with the children.

By evening, the cafeteria had become a makeshift hospital. Everyone still alive crowded into that tiny space, afraid of what the night might bring. No one had the courage to venture out on the roads. Emily was stuck in the mission. She had tried using her cell phone earlier to call Simon but there was no coverage. The mission phone lines were down, too. They waited.

The heat of the morning brought the stench of rotting bodies. There was a heated debate, but in the end they decided that the only thing they could do was cremate the bodies. They didn't have enough manpower to bury them all. Years later, Emily and Macherie would still wake up in the middle of the night with the smell of burning flesh fresh in their nostrils.

Jeffrey heard about the massacre through diplomatic channels. He knew Emily was in Nigeria but didn't know where. He called Simon.

" Well, if it isn't my favorite Roman."

"You're sounding chipper. I take it that Emily made it back all right."

"She's not due in until tomorrow."

"Have you spoken with her?"

"Actually, I tried to call about an hour ago but she's probably not at the hotel. Her phone is out of range."

"Where did you say she was going?"

When Simon told Jeff, the silence was suddenly deafening.

"Jeff? Are you there? Hello?"

Simon heard Jeff take a deep breath. "Simon. Don't panic but…there's been an attack of some sort in that general area, a mission village. The news just came in over the wires."

The minute Jeffrey said the word mission, Simon felt his blood turn to ice. He remembered his last conversation with his wife. She had said she was going to the local mission for an English class. Simon started hyperventilating.

"No…no…no…Jeff…I…*no!* It's not…it can't…Emily."

"Don't fall to pieces on me, buddy. Call the agency and see if they've heard anything and then try calling Emily again. I'll see what I can find out at this end."

For the next three days, the men didn't sleep. Babette came to stay at the house. The children knew something was up when their mother didn't come back as planned, but Simon did his best to play down the gravity of the situation, as much for himself as for the children.

The news coming out of Nigeria wasn't promising. The men were now certain that Emily had gone to the mission. Her things were still in her hotel room, and she hadn't checked out. No one could get in touch with the mission. The roads were blocked by the rebels, and all communication lines had been cut off, in part because the government didn't want much information to get out of the country. Simon and Jeff began using their connections to see what could be done.

At 5:00 a.m. on the third day, Jeff called Simon.

"Get your toothbrush. You're flying in."

"Wha…?"

"The Red Cross is going in, and I've made arrangements for you to go with them. You're booked on a flight out of Heathrow. You'll be in Lagos tonight."

Jeff then proceeded to give Simon all of the other details he needed to hook up with his contacts at the Red Cross. He would be met at the airport. As he hung up, Jeff tried to make light of the whole thing.

"You lucky dog. You get to ride in a helicopter."

"Jeff..."

"Oh, just come home alive and bring Emily back with you. And would you please tell her from me that if she ever does this to us again I'm going to sic my puppy on her?"

"I'll call you just as soon as I can."

They could see the smoke from the air. As the helicopter landed, they could see the pit of burning bodies. The air reeked of kerosene and charred, burned flesh. A small stack of bodies still waited to be thrown on the pit. Simon thought he was going to faint. One young volunteer got off the helicopter and started throwing up. Simon was already running. The first person he met was a young priest who only spoke French. Simon tried to make himself understood but he was having trouble concentrating. His eyes kept roaming desperately in search of Emily. His brain vaguely registered that the priest was indicating a low building two hundred feet away. Simon thanked him and began running toward the building. "Please, dear God," he prayed sincerely for the first time. "Let her be alive."

When he burst through the door, all of the children started screaming. Emily turned with a start, nearly fainting. She was in his arms before her brain even had time to register the fact that he was truly there. It took her several minutes to realize that they were both crying. Simon moved to get closer to his wife, but something was blocking his foot. He stepped back a second and found himself staring down into Macherie's enormous doe-like eyes. Emily quickly stooped down to scoop her up. Macherie threw her arms around Emily's neck, squeezing tightly.

"Simon...she's...I...I can't leave her." Emily's eyes pleaded with Simon, trying to transmit everything she had seen and gone through in the past few days. Simon could sense the pain. He pulled his wife gently toward him and delicately reached out to caress Macherie's tiny head.

"What's her name?" he asked softly.

"Macherie." Emily whispered

"Ma cherie." He kissed the top of his wife's head. *My daughter*, he thought to himself. It was that simple.

No one seemed surprised when he handed Emily and Macherie into the helicopter. The pilot would have loaded everyone into his cockpit if he could have. They had heard and seen enough to convince them that anyone who had lived through what they had deserved special treatment.

That night in the hotel in Lagos, after Macherie had been put to sleep, Simon and Emily made love. They came at each other like dogs in heat, changing positions several times in the course of things. Neither one of them could get close enough to the other. Each tried to express emotions through intense physical contact. After an hour they both lay spent, clinging to each other. They drifted off to sleep.

Simon was the first to wake in the morning. As he went to kiss his wife, he noticed the tiny black ball curled tightly against her side. It was Macherie. He reached out again to gently caress his daughter's head. He turned back to watch his wife's sleeping face with awe. He had fantasized about their having children once upon a time. Leave it to Emily to find a way to give him everything his heart desired. It didn't matter that he wasn't the biological father. He wanted the experience of raising a child with Emily, of having a common person to nurture and love. He bent down to kiss his wife. She stirred. He put a finger on her lips and indicated Macherie. Emiliy smiled. Macherie was sleeping soundly.

"We could try moving to her bed," she said softly.

Very carefully, Emily slid away from Macherie's side. They watched a minute with bated breath to see if she would wake up. She didn't stir. They quietly moved to the adjoining room where they were able to say good morning properly.

It took them three months to settle all of the paperwork to take Macherie out of Nigeria. It helped that she didn't have an official birth certificate. Simon was able to declare himself the natural father. There was no one to say otherwise. Everyone collaborated with them to make it happen. There was a moment when the couple almost thought they were going to have to admit defeat in front of the Nigerian bureaucracy. Emily was on the verge of collapse. She spoke to the children at home every day. She had never been away from them for this length of time. Finally, the British Consulate called them to pick up Macherie's passport. It was time to go home.

Jeff flew up to London to meet them. When the two men met at the airport, they just hugged each other and held tight. Jeff hugged Emily, too, encompassing Macherie, who still clung to Emily like a second layer of skin. Emily had never seen Jeff at a loss for words. It was moving.

When they got to the house, it was Emily's turn to be overcome with emotion. Ben had flown in from Italy. Emily hugged the children to her and burst into tears. She had come very close to never seeing them again.

Everyone made a fuss over Macherie. The children were delighted at the idea of a new sister and, knowing the story behind her arrival, wanted to make sure she knew they considered her a member of the family. The days that followed were like Christmas and Easter all rolled into one. Emily was on an emotional roller coaster, laughing one minute, crying the next, as the stress and relief from her ordeal took their toll. Simon never left her side. He was her rock, and she clung to him for support. Life gradually returned to normal.

Simon convinced Emily to quit her job. It wasn't difficult. Macherie needed her. It was an entirely new experience for Emily to be a stay-at-home mom. She loved the time spent with Macherie, but as Macherie overcame her initial trauma and was able to go to school, Emily was afraid she would get bored. It never happened. Babette drew Emily into her circle of cultural societies. She and Simon were often home in the afternoons and would go for long walks. On rainy days, they would curl up on the couch reading books. Occasionally, in the evening, Simon would put some music on, pulling Emily into his arms to dance with him. Macherie usually danced with them. They tried to get Toby to join them, but he was a full-fledged teenager and refused to be corrupted.

When Toby ran away from home, Emily thought she would have a heart attack. It was a Friday, and he simply never came home from school. By 10:00 p.m., Emily was so fraught that Simon made her drink a large shot of brandy. Unused to drinking as she was, it went straight to her head and she dozed off. At about 1:00 a.m., the phone rang. It was the father of one of Toby's friends. Toby was sleeping at their house. He had gone to Stansted to try to get on a flight to Italy but, not yet sixteen, he was still too young to fly alone. He had wandered around the airport until late at night and then had gone to his friend's house looking for a place to sleep. Simon made arrangements to pick Toby up in the morning.

The next morning Simon got up early and went to get Toby. Toby was still sleeping so the two men talked. Simon asked him whether or not Toby had given them any indications on why he had run away. The best they could get out of him was that he was feeling somehow left out at home. Simon meditated on that while he waited for Toby to wake up. Toby wasn't really surprised to see Simon when he came down to breakfast. Simon was very laid-back.

"I won't take you back home if you don't want to go, but why don't you grab something to eat and then you and I can go for a walk? I'll wait outside."

Toby joined Simon after a few minutes. The two began walking in silence. Simon decided he was going to have to do most of the talking.

"I'm probably not going to do this very well, but I don't think any parent would. It's always a new experience trying to adjust as you grow up. Toby, I honestly don't know if you realize just how important a part of my life you are to me. If you leave, you're going to take a piece of me away with you. I know that's going to happen sooner or later anyway. Ben is in Italy. Erica is at Cambridge. You're growing up. It's all just a bit too fast. I know it's selfish, but I was hoping we could keep you with us for awhile longer. If it were up to your mother and I, we would keep you at home forever. I'm just sorry you're not happy because I really love you and I want you to be happy. You're going to have to tell me if there's anything I can do to make things better for you at home?"

They had stopped walking and stood staring at each other. Simon watched as a tide of emotions flowed across Toby's face, tears appearing in his eyes.

"It's just that…Macherie gets to…call you dad and…I can't. I don't have a father!"

The emotion that welled up from Simon's feet and overtook him was so strong that he threw his arms around Toby and held on as if his life depended on it. When he thought he could speak without losing control of his voice, he loosened his grip and looked Toby in the face so that Toby could see the sincerity.

"Toby, I don't have any *biological* right to call you son, but that's what you are to me. I would be honored if you felt you could call me dad. Nothing would make me happier." He enunciated the words carefully, "You…are…my…son." Toby threw his arms around Simon and began to cry. After a few moments of holding him like that, Simon squeezed him tightly and then let go. "Come on. Your mother is beside herself with worry."

When Toby and Simon walked through the door, Emily threw her arms around her son. "Toby! Do you have any idea…?"

She would have said more but Simon silenced her with a look that said, *We'll talk later.*

Emily hugged her son tighter. "Promise me you'll never do it again."

Toby nodded and kissed his mother clumsily before shuffling upstairs to his room.

Emily hugged Simon. "Thank you."

Simon was reminded of his long-ago conversation with Jeff and smiled. What had he said? *Thank you* was nice. So was *I love you.*

"I love you." Simon said, kissing the top of her head.

Life quickly fell back into its usual pattern until the phone rang one morning at 4:00 a.m. Simon picked it up. It took him awhile to place the voice. The man said his name was Riccardo and he wanted to speak to Emily. It was Emily's ex-husband, and he sounded distressed.

"She's sleeping."

"Please. It's about Ben. There's...there's an accident."

Simon felt his blood turn to ice for the second time in his life.

"Ben? Is he all right?"

"I need to say to Emily." The tone in his voice spoke urgency. Simon took the cordless over to the bed and gently woke Emily up.

"Em. It's Riccardo. It's about Ben."

"Ben?" Emily was awake immediately. She took the phone and switched to Italian. "Pronto?"

As she listened, her face turned white. She began shaking like a leaf and her head started twitching back and forth. Simon put his arms around her. He couldn't hear what the other man was saying but he knew it wasn't good. Then Emily started screaming and writhing in pain; the phone slipping to the floor. She tried to throw herself out of Simon's arms but he refused to let her go.

"Emily. For the love of God. What's wrong? What's happened?"

All Emily could do was wail, "My baby. My beautiful baby." Over and over again. Ben was dead.

Beautiful, easygoing Ben. The apple of everyone's eye was gone. It wasn't until the day of the funeral that Simon was able to get the full story. Ben had gone to a friend's house for the evening. On his way home, a drunken driver, running through the stoplight at the intersection, hit Ben on his Vespa, sending him flying into a nearby lamppost where his spine wrapped around the pole like paper on a stick of gum. The man had been going at an incredible speed, even by Italian standards. Ben never made it to the hospital.

When they got back from Italy, Emily had to undergo testing. Her eyesight had suddenly taken a severe turn for the worse, and she was having trouble breathing, dizzy spells, chest pains. The tests all came back normal. The doctors said it was stress and that it would get better over time. Only her eyesight wouldn't improve. The damage caused by the stress was permanent. It had taken them months to find the right prescription glasses, but Emily was now wearing state-of-the-art lenses. More powerful lenses were impossible to find on the market. The prospects for the future were that Emily would gradually lose vision.

It was three years before any of them felt up to celebrating one of Jeff's outlandish Christmases, but Jeff had insisted. He and Fatima were returning to Istanbul. This was going to be their last occasion to do Christmas in Rome. Simon thought it would be good for all of them. Not that they had spent every waking moment in mourning. Macherie was seven and becoming a vivacious fun-loving creature. It was impossible to ignore her youthful enthusiasm for life. Erica and Toby had been drawn to her, too, and spent as much time as possible at home.

When he brought the subject of Christmas up with Emily, he was pleased that she readily agreed, especially because Jeffrey had inadvertently reminded him of the debt they owed him when he had jokingly said, "I've finally paid all those favors back for Emily's divorce and now they're kicking me out of the country."

They were all looking forward to Christmas in Rome, so when Fatima called, it took them all by surprise. Jeffrey had had a heart attack. Emily took the call. She listened quietly as Fatima told her the news.

"I'm so sorry, Fatima. I'll tell Simon."

Fatima had then given her all of the details for the funeral. Emily hung up the phone and allowed herself a few quiet moments of grief. She took a deep breath and went to tell Simon, steeling herself for his pain.

Simon was in the living room playing with Macherie when Emily walked into the room.

"Macherie, honey, would you go and get Toby for me? Tell him to use the five-minute rule." The five-minute rule was a secret code between Toby and his mother. It meant that Toby was supposed to keep his sister occupied for as long as possible so that Emily could do something, usually organize a surprise party or discuss something she didn't want Macherie to hear. Macherie ran off obediently calling out, "Toby! Five minutes!!"

Simon remained on the couch, looking questioningly at his wife. The expression on her face made him uneasy, and he could see that she had been crying. She sat down next to him and took his hand in hers.

"That was Fatima. Jeff had a heart attack last night."

Simon felt a lump form in the pit of his stomach. Emily looked into his eyes and her expression gave him the answer he was dreading to his unspoken question.

It was like letting the air out of a balloon. Simon simply caved in on himself.

Emily threw her arms around him. "Oh Simon, I'm so sorry."

Simon gently pushed her back and got unsteadily to his feet and headed to their bedroom, closing the door behind him. Emily followed. It was her turn to be strong for him. He had thrown himself across the bed, his arm over his eyes. His body was heaving as he fought against the tears. Emily lay down next to him, trying delicately to pull his head toward her chest, whispering softly, "I can pull the plaster model out if you'd rather have a firmer bosom to comfort you."

The tears flowed freely after that. Simon wrapped his arms tightly around Emily, letting himself sink into the abysses of his sorrow, certain that she would somehow keep him from drowning.

Life is a sequence of emotions like sheet music that we all draw randomly at birth and must learn to play. Some of us live ragtime lives, others jazz. A few unfortunate souls are forced to interpret complex blues. It isn't ours to define the sequence of notes on the pages of our life, the rhythm, the pauses, the tempo. Our only ability is in the expression, our interpretation of the music as it unfolds. Emily and Simon were lucky to have both drawn a sonata. The changes in tempo mirroring the changes in their lives, now fast, now slow, now lively, now sad, but always continuous, a single composition in more than one part; perhaps more incredibly, their interpretations were flawless and perfectly matched.

k e haines

Encore

Emily sighed and gave up looking at herself in the mirror. She was just going to have to take Erica's word that she looked radiant. She felt radiant. Simon, as if reading her thoughts, came up behind her, taking her shoulders and gently turning her around to face him.

"You look beautiful tonight."

Emily's face softened into her familiar expression of love. Simon kissed her gently on the lips.

"I have something for you."

"Simon. I thought we agreed no presents. Isn't this cruise enough?"

"I didn't buy you a present." He took a thin box from his inner jacket pocket and placed it in her hands.

Emily took the box and slowly lifted the lid. Nestled against the dark blue lining was a simple strand of pearls with a very intricate rose clasp.

"These are the pearls my father gave my mother on their twenty-fifth wedding anniversary. I've been saving them for the occasion. Happy anniversary." Simon spoke softly to control his emotions.

Emily felt her eyes grow moist as she delicately removed the pearls from their box. They were magnificent.

"Here, let me put them on." Simon took the pearls from Emily and fastened the necklace around her neck, the rose in front.

"There are fifty of them. My father always told my mother that there was one for each year they'd been together and one for each year he'd live all over again with her if he could."

Emily chuckled softly. "Can you imagine what would have happened if the jeweler had miscounted?"

Simon smiled and caressed his wife's cheek with the back of his hand. "Dad was a stickler for detail. It wouldn't have happened."

"I love you."

"I love you, too."

Their lips met, and for awhile neither one of them spoke. Simon was the first to pull back.

"We'd better go. The children will be waiting."

"Especially because if you continue to kiss me like that I'm going to have to dig Jeff's dental gel out of the suitcase and then we'll really be late."

Simon smiled fondly. "Jeff thought of everything. He would have loved this cruise."

Emily reached up and cupped his head in her hand. "Of course he would have. Jeffrey loved celebrations, and life was meant to be celebrated."

Simon took his wife's hand and kissed her palm then, weaving his fingers into hers. They left their cabin hand in hand. When they got to the restaurant, they discovered that they were the first to arrive. Just as they were about to sit down, the band began playing "No Woman, No Cry." Simon pulled Emily to the dance floor. They were still dancing when Toby, his wife Sheila, their son Simon, and Macherie with her fiancé walked into the room.

Toby turned to his sister. "Hey. Cherie. Did you remember to bring your camera?"

Macherie handed him the camera and he took the picture. They all crowded around to look at the shot in the view window. He had captured them at just the right moment. Emily's upturned face, Simon's intense expression as he gazed into her eyes; the poignancy of the image left them all silent for a moment.

"I think this is how I'll always remember them."

"Remember who?" Erica and her husband had come up from behind. Toby handed her the camera to look at the picture. She and her husband bent over to examine the shot and then showed it to their son Ben. The music ended.

"Come on. Let's go and show it to them," Macherie said, holding her hand out for the camera.

Ben ventured, "Maybe we could get it enlarged and frame it for them for Christmas so that grandma can see it properly."

"That's a good idea, Ben. Hey, Cherie," Erica called after her sister, who was already halfway across the room. "Don't show it to Dad yet. It'll be a nice surprise for both of them."

They all moved forward together. Simon, who was helping Emily into her seat, caught sight of them and waved. They all smiled in acknowledgment, the grandchildren rushing ahead, impatient to start the festivities.

www.ingramcontent.com/pod-product-compliance
Lightning Source LLC
Chambersburg PA
CBHW021119130626
46554CB00002B/781